A LITTLE MISS TAKEN

A LITTLE MISS TAKEN

THE FIRST BOBBIE FLYNN MYSTERY

JACK MURRAY

Books by Jack Murray

Kit Aston Mysteries.
The Affair of the Christmas Card Killer
The Chess Board Murders.
The Phantom
Museum
The Frisco Falcon
The Medium Murders
The Bluebeard Club
The Tangier Tajine
The Empire Theatre Murders
The Newmarket Murders
The New Year's Eve Murders
The French Diplomat Affair (novella)
Haymaker's Last Fight (novelette)

DI Jellicoe Mysteries
A Time to Kill
The Bus Stop
Trio
Dolce Vita Murders

Agatha Aston Mysteries
Black-Eyed Nick
The Witchfinder General Murders
The Christmas Murder Mystery
The Siegfried Slayer (Oct 2023)

Danny Shaw / Manfred Brehme WWII Series
The Shadow of War
Crusader
El Alamein

The Bobbie Flynn Mysteries
A Little Miss Taken
Murder on Tin Pan Alley
Murder at the Metropolitan

Copyright © 2024 by Jack Murray

All rights reserved. No part of this publication may be reproduced, distributed, or transmitted in any form or by any means, including photocopying, recording, or other electronic or mechanical methods, without the prior written permission of the publisher, except in the case of brief quotations embodied in critical reviews and certain other non-commercial uses permitted by copyright law. For permission requests, write to the publisher, addressed 'Attention: Permissions Coordinator,' at the address below.

Jackmurray99@hotmail.com

This is a work of fiction. Names, characters, businesses, places, events, locales, and incidents are either the products of the author's imagination or used in a fictitious manner. Any resemblance to actual persons, living or dead, or actual events is purely coincidental.

Cover by Jack Murray

ISBN: 9798320805467
Imprint: Independently published

For Monica, Lavinia, Anne and our angel baby, Edward….

1

Offices of the New York American, Park Street, New York: 2nd January 1922

New York, on New Year's Eve 1921, glittered like a diamond in a police searchlight the night Amory Beaufort was murdered.

Bobbie Flynn looked at her typewriter and smiled to herself. She liked the line she had just typed. She liked it a lot in fact. Then a cold feeling enveloped her. What would Thornton Kent think? All at once her confidence ebbed away. Perhaps it was too dramatic. Hyperbole. He hated hyperbole. Except of course when it was Damon. Or Amory when he had been alive. Yes, when men like that handed in their work it was as if Shakespeare himself had entered the offices of the *New York American* coining epigrams and sonnets to grateful sub-editors in need of intellectual stimulation.

The thought of her colleagues or, at least, the former colleague, sent a surge of anger which throbbed from her temple and down through her arms to fingers that began to type rapidly on the keys. The words flew from the keys to the paper at a dizzying pace propelled by a rage that was only partially attributable to her auburn-red locks and Irish roots.

Twenty minutes later the report was finished and she reviewed it grimly. In her estimation, and she was her own worst critic, the piece was well written, concise, with sufficient

1

human interest from someone who had been an eyewitness to a murder and his capture.

Bobbie Flynn had, only a couple of days earlier, attended a party, a murder mystery party no less, where the host had become a victim. Thanks to the presence of her father, an inspector with the New York Police Department and a few unusual English people who had a peculiar knack for detection, they had ensured that the murderer was identified within hours of the killing taking place. Of course, such things are only possible when English amateur detectives are involved. It begs the question why, with such a strikingly high success rate, they are not used more often in criminal investigations the world over.

She read the report twice. The first time was to see how it felt. To Bobbie, it felt just right. The second time was to check for grammar and punctuation lest some punctilious sub-editors reject a superb article on the basis of her heinous misuse of a comma, mid clause.

One of the attributes possessed by women, sorely lacking in chaps, is that they are infinitely more collaborative by nature. Perhaps this is a misplaced lack of confidence in their own capability or a desire not to repeat the mistakes of their male colleagues, who are singularly devoid of humility, when it comes to assessing their own competence.

Bobbie decided, rather as a good doctor might, to obtain a second opinion. She glanced into an office where her immediate boss, Buckner Fanley, sat scowling over a newspaper. A scowl was set permanently on the countenance of the newspaper's head of obituaries. This may have been ascribed to the serious nature of the columns that he oversaw, but to those who knew and invariably disliked him, this was, in fact, a permanent feature.

To describe him as 'head' was a vast overstatement of what was a small team. It comprised him and Bobbie. They detested one another and made no secret of this fact. Fanley saw Bobbie as a *parvenu* who only regarded obituaries as a stepping stone to fashion, household tips or whatever it was that interested the female of the species. Meanwhile, Bobbie had to endure the role of office dogsbody as Fanley allowed her to do the bulk of the research on the recently deceased and prospective clients, or not, for entry to Paradise. The latter work was particularly morbid as the paper had to ensure its library of obits was up to date with latest news on the not-yet-deceased. Of course, Fanley was happy to put his name to Bobbie's work. All in all, their relationship simmered like the surface of a geyser.

Bobbie rose from her seat and ignored the sharp jerk of Fanley's head as he glanced up at his attractive young assistant walking past the office window. Bobbie gritted her teeth and headed for the open area where many of the reporters sat. She knew that every man Jack of them would stop what they were doing and watch her pass along the rows of desks.

What was going on in their minds, as they looked at her, did not bear thinking about. Thankfully, everyone in the office knew that her father was a police inspector, a rather well-known one, in fact. This acted as a form of protection against the unwanted attentions of prospective middle-aged Lotharios who could probably still teach a young girl a thing or two given the chance, or so they claimed.

At the far end of the office was Thornton Kent's office. She could see the all-powerful editor pacing the room like a lion caged in a wardrobe. He didn't look happy, but then again, he never did. Bobbie's eyes darted over to a table by the window that was set aside for the man that she had come to see.

Damon Runyon.

Runyon was the golden boy of the newspaper, although at forty years of age, while he was no longer a shooting star, he was certainly the shining jewel in the newspaper's firmament. His fame stretched beyond the sweaty confines of the newsroom, beyond even New York, to the rest of the country thanks to his sports writing, in particular his writing about baseball and boxing.

Bobbie's eyes fell on the slender writer, crouched over his typewriter like an angry parent with a recalcitrant child. Ignoring the leering eyes of the other men in the room, Bobbie made straight for her friend and sometime drinking buddy. Her familiarity with Broadway's speakeasies and criminal element almost matched that of Runyon. This was something that she tended to keep quiet from her policeman father who, not unreasonably, would have taken a dim view both professionally and parentally of such associations.

Perhaps your chronicler is biased, but men are genuinely amazing creatures. Whether it is due to the good Lord's sense of humour or a remarkable by-product of a few million years of evolution, but the male genus of *homo sapiens* has an in-built alarm for whenever an attractive woman is in the vicinity. Although Bobbie was not yet several tables away, and despite the fact that he was facing in another direction, Runyon glanced around and viewed the approaching young woman with undisguised pleasure.

He was a connoisseur of women, beautiful women preferably, although he had a penchant for funny women in particular. Bobbie Flynn qualified on all three counts in his book. This liking had never been sullied by any impropriety on Runyon's part beyond introducing her to some unusual Broadway characters and even more unusual cocktails.

'Red,' exclaimed Runyon, calling Bobbie by the name she was commonly known in the newsroom. 'What's cookin'?'

Bobbie waved a couple of typed sheets in his direction.

'Do you know that unpaid job you have as my proof reader?' she said with a grin.

Runyon scowled back at her without any malice, 'You use my good nature.'

'Would you prefer if it I used your body?' said Bobbie, just loud enough to make several middle-aged reporters in the vicinity groan.

Runyon, picking up on the thread left dangling by Bobbie, countered, 'It's over kid. We had some laughs but move on.'

A few eyebrows in the room shot up at this. They knew of Runyon's penchant for younger women, but this would have been the ultimate scoop.

Runyon had worked his way up from small town journalism in Pueblo, Colorado to the pinnacle of New York news. He did so because he understood that the nature of news was ephemeral; its purpose was to grab the attention of readers and this could best be achieved by reporting what happened in the bedroom, on the sports field or by a police desk.

Moments later, Runyon was on his feet cackling his smokers laugh. He hugged Bobbie and took the sheets of paper from her hand.

'Give me those, honey,' he said while sitting down to read. Bobbie perched on his desk and stared over him. Almost immediately he began to laugh. This is rarely a good sign and Runyon confirmed this a moment later.

'It's a good line, but he'll never let it through,' said Runyon.

'Can't you say anything?'

'Why should I when I might steal it myself?'

'Beast,' laughed Bobbie.

'I'll see what I can do.'

Runyon read in semi-silence. There was the odd grumble along the way and his pen circled dangerously over the page like a bird of prey but did not swoop down to deliver its damning verdict. Finally, Runyon looked up. He smiled.

'It's good Red, but Kent will throw a fit. You know he will,' observed Runyon.

'Will you take out a few things and…'

'…and you'll tell Kent that Damon had helped you. Nice idea. Might work. Once.'

Runyon brandished his pen, received a nod from Bobbie and then it descended like Madame La Guillotine to do its gruesome work. Bobbie watched the red flow and it felt as if she was being repeatedly stabbed. She steeled herself as she saw some of her best work butchered by her friend, but it was for a good cause.

A couple of minutes later she surveyed the carnage. Yet, when she read the article, miraculously it was still coherent and, heartbreakingly, probably better for the surgery that Runyon had performed. Whether the patient would make a full recovery remained to be seen. She glanced in the direction of Thornton Kent's office.

Butterflies battered the walls of her stomach as she prepared herself to march in and do battle for her story. Kent was aware that she was an eyewitness to a murder that had shocked the whole of the newsroom as it involved a sometime colleague, Amory Beaufort. Reluctantly, he had acceded to Bobbie's demand that she get to write the story. He had done so on the proviso that she make a decent stab at it. He'd laughed at his intentional pun.

Bobbie wanted to run from the office, yet it was too late now. The whole of the newsroom was pretending not to be aware of the drama about to play out. The drama that might end in her walking out on her dream of being a crime reporter. These were the stakes and it felt as if everyone in the room knew this.

She was holding her breath as she hoped to catch the eye of the editor. At last, he looked up. Unerringly his eyes went straight to Bobbie. Or perhaps it was the shock of reddish-auburn hair that caught his attention.

With a single, graceful movement he waved at her to come in.

Bobbie sailed over towards the office stopping long enough to say, 'Hi Skinny', to a man that resembled a walrus complete with a handlebar moustache.

Behind her Runyon said, 'Good luck Red,' in a low voice. And meant it.

2

Somewhere in central casting, probably one of the main commandments is a requirement that New York newspaper editors be pugnacious, cigar-chewing middle-aged men who were born in a sweat-stained shirt with the sleeves rolled up. Thornton Kent was just such a man. In fact, he was so like this that he was virtually a caricature for the breed.

He had seen the arrival of Bobbie Flynn a few minutes earlier, as every man within a fifteen-yard radius had, but unlike the other men, he had felt paradoxically a sinking heart and his temper rise. This is no mean feat in any man and was further evidence of the perfect alignment between the man and the career he had chosen.

Noting that she, at least, had the sense to speak to Runyon first, he waved her in. He trusted Damon Runyon. And why wouldn't he? He was one of the highest paid newsmen in the city, if not the highest. William Randolph Hearst, the newspaper owner, was a fan and had been prepared to pay top dollar to keep him from the clutches of other papers. If he passed the young woman's report as fit for publishing, then who was he to argue?

But where was the fun in not having a fight?

Bobbie Flynn entered the office and Kent could see immediately the fear in her face. He could almost smell it.

How would she react when he started to do what he always did in such a situation?

Terrify them more.

'What do you want?' he barked at Bobbie as she stepped hesitantly towards his desk.

'Here's the report you asked for,' said Bobbie. Her voice was steady, as was her gaze, he observed. This was a good sign. Whatever nervousness she felt had been rapidly brought under control. Time to test if this would hold.

'What report?' barked Kent, pretending to be genuinely mystified although he did have a memory of asking her to report on something. He glared at Bobbie.

In situations such as this, one either melts into the ground under the heat of the gaze or you find something within you to fight back. Once more, anger came to Bobbie's aid. She marched over to Kent's desk, leaned over it in a manner that was aggressive by any standard and slammed the report down in front of him.

'You know fine well Mr Kent. This is my eyewitness account of Amory's murder.'

As it happened, Kent had remembered just as the sheaf of papers came crashing down below his nose.

'Do you know the only thing that's stopping me from ripping this thing in two and sending you back to your pops?' snarled Kent, rising to his feet.

Bobbie was too committed now to shrink back so she held her ground and stared right back at the newspaper editor. They stayed like this for a few moments until Bobbie realised that she had been asked a question.

'What?' asked Bobbie, recovering herself.

'Nothing,' replied Kent. Then he leaned forward menacingly. 'Out,' he yelled and pointed to the open door.

Bobbie decided that she had prevailed enough on his good nature and swiftly exited the office. One newsman called Pete Harris, whom she had referred to as "Skinny" earlier, glanced up and grinned at her as she passed him.

'You caught him in a good mood, Red,' said Harris.

Bobbie laughed at this and said, 'I'd hate to see what he's like when he's in a foul temper.'

She glanced over at Damon Runyon who gave her a wink before returning his attention to his own typewriter. A cigarette hung in his mouth with a long strip of ash in danger of toppling forward.

Bobbie was glad to leave the smoke-stained atmosphere of the newsroom and reach the corridor. There was nothing else to do but to go to the office she shared with Fanley. It was a large office, by any standard. It housed an enormous library of old newspapers and filing cabinets of obituaries of the dead or soon-to-be dead.

While she may have been glad to leave the maleness of the newsroom, the office where she worked was hardly more welcoming. Her boss, Buckner Fanley and she, had an uneasy relationship. He had opposed her taking the job but had since come to accept that she worked hard, wrote crisply without much need for him to edit, although he did so because it irritated her and amused him.

Fanley had spent the last ten years working in "Obits" and the rather morbid nature of the job had long since rubbed off on a personality that was one part martinet and one part zombie. For the most part, he was ignored by the rest of the newspaper staff but, oddly, Thornton Kent rather liked him.

They made an odd pair. Kent was big, charismatic and loud. Fanley was small, cadaverous with an undisguised dislike of most people, something that was happily reciprocated.

Fanley observed the arrival of Bobbie through his round, rimless glasses. Bobbie noticed his gaze and returned it with interest.

'So?' began Fanley. 'Did he take your report?' There was just enough hint of Fanley's natural sneer to irritate Bobbie.

As much as she would like to have replied that he had taken it, read it and immediately decided that she deserved a place on the crime desk, that would have stretched a child's credulity.

'You tell me,' replied Bobbie sourly. 'I mean, he has one of his own reporters...'

'You work in obituaries, this is hardly reporting,' pointed out Fanley with a mirthless smile.

'Don't remind me.'

'No one is pointing a gun to your head, like Hamilton Monk,' snapped Fanley. This was a reference to a rich banker who had committed suicide just before Christmas.

Bobbie ignored the jibe and slumped down on her seat. She had the unenviable task of writing a small obituary for Amory Beaufort, a man that she had considered a friend until she had discovered only a couple of days previously that he had been involved in a murder-suicide pact with a young woman who had been killed, while he had lived. Then he had been murdered himself.

Bobbie's initial anger with Amory Beaufort had passed and she was left with a nagging sense of guilt that she had not seen the real man behind the, admittedly good-looking, mask. He had been a friend to her. Had she been one to him?

'Leave the Beaufort obituary to me,' said Fanley, which surprised Bobbie and left her feeling grateful towards her boss. This was never a good feeling, and it immediately irritated her. Before Bobbie could offer anything by way of thanks, Fanley added quickly, 'I want you to go to the Monk townhouse, up near Central Park. They've asked that we write a sympathetic piece about their dear departed father. They don't want a life that was spent acquiring pots of money to be sullied by his rather bloody end. See if you can find something nice to say about him. His bank advertised in our paper and we want them to continue doing so.'

Bobbie nodded at this before replying, 'Did he really commit suicide?' she asked. 'I remember my dad mentioned that they were investigating it.'

'Really?' sneered Fanley. 'Your father must be losing touch. The inquest declared suicide on New Year's Eve.'

Any insult towards her father was always guaranteed to send Bobbie's temperature gauge soaring.

'I'm sure he was aware but did not mention it to me,' retorted Bobbie. 'It's not like he discusses every case with me.'

'A crime-fighting reporter like you? I'd have thought he would want to draw upon your great experience and powers of deduction as often as possible.'

There was no point in talking to the horrible man when he was in this mood, so Bobbie rose to her feet and snapped back at him, 'When do they want to see me?'

'Now.'

'Address?'

'Do you see that thing in front of you. It's white, rectangular and has writing on it. It's called paper...' said Fanley. The address was on her desk in front of her eyes. She grabbed it and a handbag where she kept her notebook then stalked out of the office ignoring the delighted smile of Fanley. She heard Fanley shout as she exited, 'Ask for Jefferson Monk. He's the eldest son.'

At the bottom of the stairs, she met Damon Runyon who was on his way out of the building. He grinned at her and said, 'Drink?' It was not yet eleven in the morning. Bobbie raised her eyebrows, disapprovingly, which made Runyon guffaw. 'It'll loosen you up, Red.'

'I have to go write a puff piece about Hamilton Monk,' explained Bobbie.

'He was no Monk, trust me,' laughed Runyon before saluting her on the pavement as they went their different ways.

3

The *New York American* offices were in the Tribune Building, which was situated, along with most of the New York newspaper world, on Park Row. The street that started near the entrance of Brooklyn Bridge ran at an angle for a short distance, facing City Hall Park and the City Hall itself. For years, the nine story Redstone Tribune was the tallest building in Manhattan. Its clocktower rose 285 feet in the air. The Hearst papers were published out of the second and third floors.

Bobbie shivered as she walked down the icy steps. She stopped and glanced up at the building, before walking carefully along the sidewalk to the City Hall subway, to take her up to East 69th Street. Snowflakes fluttered down gently, caressing her cheek and melting immediately. The snow had turned into a grey sludge on the path, trodden down by a thousand or so men and women. It was still a little early to go to the Monk household. She felt a gentle rumbling in her stomach and this decided her next course of action.

An hour later, which included a breakfast she'd missed when rushing to the newspaper offices to file her report and she was outside the large town house on 69th which was across the road from Central Park.

Bobbie found herself standing outside a six-story residence with a limestone and rose-brick façade with four towering pillars at the entrance. A different world thought Bobbie before it occurred to her that this was probably not even their primary residence. She remembered that they also owned a large mansion on Long Island.

Just as she was about to walk along the path leading to the front door, two little girls, both dressed in white, brushed past her. They were no older than ten years old, each had light brown hair. This is where the similarity ended.

One of the girls was elfin thin, pretty as a picture on a chocolate box, with wide blue eyes. The other was a little bigger with darker eyes and a face that seemed harder, more suspicious. She glanced suspiciously at Bobbie before taking the arm of the other and leading her towards the park across the road.

Bobbie strode forward towards the front door. She took each step carefully, fearful of any ice lurking to upend an unsuspecting visitor. The snow was piled up high, tipping over the low walls either side of the steps. She reached the large oak door and gave the bell a ring. A few moments later she was received by a liveried butler who looked like the living incarnation of Mr Pickwick.

'Good morning,' he said in an accent that was very English, but minus the pretension that Americans often associate with the island race. Bobbie decided she liked him even though they had only just met. He asked her, 'How can I help you?'

'Good morning, sir,' said Bobbie giving him her full Broadway smile. While Bobbie disliked women who played on their beauty to cast a spell over men, she wasn't beneath doing it herself, when the occasion demanded. Any hint of hypocrisy would have been stoutly countered by her view that she never used her looks to entrap men. No, it was merely for them to do her bidding. This was an altogether different thing and quite innocent, she believed.

'I have come to see Mr Monk. He requested an interview with my paper the *New York American* to talk about his late father.'

'Ah yes, he did say something about this, Miss. May I ask...?'

'Roberta Flynn,' said Bobbie deciding that just this once it might be better to use her full name. She did this on her newspaper by-line as it had a little more gravitas than Bobbie, which she loved, but made her seem like a cheerleader.

The aged butler invited Bobbie in and led her to a chair in the large entrance hallway, while he set off to find Monk. This gave Bobbie an opportunity to look around her and what she saw was mightily impressive.

The black and white tiled floor looked like something from a seventeenth century Dutch painting, something which the owner of the house was plainly aware of as there were a couple of Peter de Hooch paintings just behind where she sat. At the top of the wide stairs, which swept in a majestic curve to the tiled floor, was a large, life-sized portrait of a man that Bobbie took to be the recently-deceased, Hamilton Monk.

The man in the painting was around seventy, with his head tilted upwards in a manner that was meant to convey power and no little arrogance. At his feet was a Great Dane, with head similarly raised. Bobbie wondered if the artist was making a point about the pomposity of the sitter. Nothing in the man's obituary suggested he lacked self-assurance, egotism, or enemies.

As she gazed at the image, she wondered what had driven him to kill himself. The man in the painting seemed full of vigour and will to live. It made the rather rapid conclusion from the inquest of suicide seem strange to Bobbie.

Or perhaps she was just itching to be involved in a criminal case. The former bank chairman stared down at all who entered, from underneath dark bushy eyebrows, with all of the benign welcome of a Pit Bull Terrier disturbed from restful sleep.

After a few minutes, the old butler returned. He smiled at Bobbie and said apologetically, 'I'm afraid Mr Monk is unavoidably detained at the moment and offers his apologies. He said that if you were prepared to wait half an hour, he will be able to see you then.'

'Of course,' smiled Bobbie, who did not fancy returning to the office now that she was already here. 'Would you mind if I waited?'

'As you wish. If you'll come with me, I'll take you to the drawing room. Perhaps I can get you a tea or a coffee?'

'Thank you, a tea would be lovely,' answered Bobbie.

The drawing room was a high-ceilinged affair, replete with a grand piano, wood panelled walls and a fireplace in which Bobbie could have set up an apartment. On the wall was a Fragonard with one of his usual flirtatious young women. This was not to Bobbie's taste, although she did like Charles Dana Gibson and Nell Brinkley who, probably, were just twentieth century versions of the same.

A few minutes later, the butler arrived with the tea.

'Thank you, Mr...?' said Bobbie as the tea was placed on a side table by the armchair.

'Froome,' said the butler. 'I am Froome. If you need anything else just give that bell rope by the door a little tug.'

'I shall. But before you go, I was wondering if you could tell me something. I'm here to write a piece about the late Mr Monk. I'm sure it was a great shock to everyone in the house,' said Bobbie sympathetically.

The butler paused for a moment unsure if, after a lifetime in service, it was his place to make any comment on the people he considered his masters. An innate sense of good manners won out and he replied, 'Yes, it was a great surprise and a tragedy.'

'Had you been in service long with Mr Monk?'

'Almost eight years.'

'But you are from England, I can tell.'

'Indeed. I came over with my master, Lord Boreham, eight years ago. He had often expressed a wish to see America before he died and we travelled together to do just that,' said Froome, with a faraway tone in his voice as he remembered a sad time of his life.

'Oh, I'm so sorry Mr Froome,' said Bobbie.

'Just Froome, Miss Flynn,' smiled Froome. 'Yes, Lord Boreham passed away at the Long Island estate of Mr Monk. It was not unexpected, I must say. He had been ill for some time. Mr Monk was kind enough to offer me a position in the house and I accepted gratefully.'

Bobbie decided that to press the venerable butler any further would be a little bit too pushy after so short an acquaintance and when he had been so welcoming.

'Thank you, Mr...sorry, Froome. You've been very kind and I'm sorry if our conversation has brought back any sad memories for you.'

Froome smiled sadly but said nothing. Instead, he bowed and silently left the room. The room was very warm and exuded a quiet peace, which felt at odds with the rather overpowering entrance hallway. Bobbie sat in silence, listening to the sound of the grandfather clock echoing around the wood panelling. It felt oddly peaceful.

Within an hour, all hell would break loose.

4

Monk Townhouse, East 69^h Street, New York: 2nd January 1922

The twenty minutes before the arrival of Bobbie Flynn to the Monk townhouse had been rather a busy one for the septuagenarian butler, Froome. Barely had he led one visitor to the drawing room when the next set of visitors would be banging impatiently on the door. It was Froome's sad observation of his eight years living on the *wrong* side of the Atlantic that Americans, the male genus in particular, had all the practised patience of a five-year-old at an ice cream parlour.

Froome was philosophical about this sad state of affairs. On the one hand, it made him all the more desirous to be seen to be a force for calm, unhurried efficiency. On the other, he had a deep and abiding respect for a people that could conquer a continent and turn themselves into the most powerful nation on earth in a matter of decades. Such achievement was probably not possible if the personality of the exploring nation was marked by high patience and a wait-and-see attitude. No, he conceded, what made this country great was an act first, think later character that he rather admired.

The visitors in question were mostly family as well as a few business partners of the late, lamented Hamilton Monk. The banker had not been everyone's cup of tea. Let it not be said that he had risen to the top on the back of his personal charm and willingness to do the right thing by those around him. Froome was under no illusions about Mr Monk. The man was now, and Froome suspected, a depositor in that great fiery vault below.

Yet for all this, Froome had rather liked the old man. And he felt that this was reciprocated. This was because they were of a similar vintage if not outlook. The first thing Monk had said to him when he and Lord Boreham had come to stay was to call him Pickwick. Froome had said nothing about this as it was something he had heard many times before. The only thing that made it noteworthy was his astonishment that Monk was familiar with Dickens.

Another point in favour of old man Monk was his kindly treatment of Lord Boreham. For this alone Froome would have done anything for the banker even while he had to bear witness to his otherwise capricious, unforgiving and avaricious nature. And these were just his good points.

Jefferson Monk sat in his dining room and watched people file in. Beside him was the family lawyer Fitzroy Belmont. Belmont had taken over from his father, Pitt Belmont, to head up Belmont, Belmont & Fisher. The firm had handled the legal affairs of the Monks for decades and there was no reason to assume that this would not remain the case for the next few decades. He hoped.

The new head of Monk & Marsh was Jefferson Monk. This would be confirmed in a few minutes by Belmont. This much Monk knew. However, rather frustratingly, his family's lawyer had been more circumspect about the rest of the old man's will. A part of him respected the fact that Fitzroy had said nothing, but at least, for old times' sake, he might have said something to reassure him about what they were about to hear.

Monk watched his wife and brother sit down to his left followed by two cousins from South Carolina who he and his siblings heartily detested, Elspeth and Lawrence Beauregard. They were from their mother's side of the family. The Beauregard family had fought the North in the Civil War against people like the Monks. They never let you forget it either, thought Monk. You took our money, they complained. This was not an accusation levelled against the Monk family in particular so much as a complaint about the treatment of the South following the war. Fifty years on and it was still not over for some.

Half a dozen of the staff from the house, and also the Long Island estate, were the last to file into the dining room. Fitzroy Belmont looked up at the throng in the room, adjusted his spectacles, and glanced towards Monk. A barely perceptible nod came from his friend. He cleared his throat and lifted a sheaf of papers.

Froome watched the proceedings with a rather jaundiced eye. He was not expecting much, and he did not mind. He knew that Monk had provided for him in the only way that mattered. He would be allowed to stay for as long as he wished in the servant's quarters at the Long Island mansion. Nothing else mattered to Froome. He was in his seventies now. A place to live, a warm fire and his pipe were all he needed. The others around him, particularly the family were a little more hopeful, he suspected.

He glanced towards Mrs Theodora Monk, Jefferson's wife. Teddy was beautiful and malevolent in equal measure. To her left was Quincy Monk, the raffish younger brother of Jefferson. The lawyer shook his head. Quincy was unshaven and looked distinctly the worse for wear. He'd obviously been to one or more of the dozens of speakeasies in Manhattan that considered him a valued customer. Quincy caught the eye of Belmont and gave him a wink. It was difficult to dislike the young man. Few did. And women loved him.

His brother, Jefferson was certainly his father's son. He felt Jefferson's eyes on him and he took that as his cue to start the proceedings: the reading of the will. There was a hum of noise in the room, although the family, at the table, sat grim-faced except for Quincy.

'If I may have your attention,' began Belmont. 'I would like to get matters underway.'

'Here, here,' murmured Quincy, who seemed to find this intervention amusing, even if no one else did. He ignored the glare from both his brother and Teddy.

Belmont, like a consummate actor, made a point of scanning the room to make sure all eyes were on him. In fact, to Froome, it seemed the eyes of the portrait of the dead patriarch, which was over the fireplace behind the lawyer, were also looking down on the proceedings.

'As you know, Belmont, Belmont,' began the proud descendant of the law firm. He continued after a pause, 'and Fisher, have had the honour of serving the Monk family for four decades. It was my father who first had the melancholy experience of drawing up the last will and testament on Mr Monk's behalf in 1891.'

Belmont paused at this point for effect. This was rather undermined by the sound of Jefferson Monk drumming his fingers on the table. Belmont decided to get to the point.

'Well, we know why we are here. That being so, with your permission, I will eliminate the preliminaries and get straight to the essential items.' And, knowing that everyone was solely interested in what they would get, he proceeded to do just that. 'The staff of the Long Island and 69th street homes shall each receive the sum of one thousand dollars, to be paid one year after the reading of this will, lest they decide to up and leave us. For dear old Froome, I leave an additional three thousand dollars and a proviso that he is allowed to spend the rest of his days in the Long Island home. I shall miss you old friend.'

All eyes turned to the old butler which caused him to look down, his face colouring in uninvited attention.

'Here, here,' said Quincy and, for once, he was not being cynical.

Belmont allowed for a few moments of appreciation for the service of Froome before resuming the reading.

'To my dear niece and nephew Elspeth and Lawrence Beauregard, I leave ten thousand dollars each. Your name means beautiful gaze, yet I have always found you ugly inside, like most of my wife's family.'

There were gasps around the room, which halted the reading momentarily. Jefferson Monk looked on impassively, but Quincy appeared to enjoy the discomfort of his cousins immensely. Meanwhile, Teddy Monk seemed close to tears. Seeing this, Jefferson took his wife's hand. This quickly wiped any sense of triumph from the face of Quincy.

Belmont continued the reading.

'To my youngest son, I leave the sum of hundred and fifty thousand dollars. This will be paid to him on his thirtieth birthday by which time I hope he will have grown up. Payment will only be made if it is the opinion of Mr Fitzroy Belmont that he has sufficient maturity to handle such a bequest and will not drink himself into an early death. Should Quincy marry and should he remain married at the age of forty, and should he be considered sober of mind as well as body, this sum will rise to two hundred thousand dollars. I won't hold my breath on this happening and, by virtue of the fact you are all sitting around a table listening to Fitzroy read, I shall be unable to do so anyway.'

It was the turn of the Beauregards to smile, as they enjoyed the discomfort of their hated cousin. Quincy tried to maintain his composure and took the opportunity to light a cigarette. Only his brother noticed that his hands shook slightly as he did so.

Belmont did not let the dead banker's words hang in the air for long, as he continued remorselessly, 'To my eldest son, Jefferson. No man could have asked for a better son to continue the family business. You shall take over my position as head of Monk & Marsh with immediate effect.'

Jefferson glanced up at a tall, slender man standing alongside the staff of the house. He was dressed expensively in a perfectly cut, dark morning suit. This was August St Clair the deputy chairman of Monk & Marsh. St Clair had always thought the bank sounded like a firm of ecclesiastical outfitters. He nodded to Jefferson. Belmont's voice distracted both men.

'To Jefferson, I bequeath the sum of two hundred and fifty thousand dollars and a further one hundred thousand dollars for my beloved granddaughter, Lydia, to be received on her twenty-first birthday.'

Jefferson Monk's face softened as he heard his beloved daughter's name read out. He felt Teddy take his hand. The old man had doted on his granddaughter and, perhaps, it was hearing her name that brought home to him that he was no longer with them.

Elspeth looked at her cousin and thought that he was a much better actor than she had given him credit for. Both cousins almost looked as if they missed the old man.

'And finally, to my dear wife Leonora, I leave my houses and all other possessions for the rest of her days. She was the light of my life and I pray that she will not miss me too greatly for we will, I earnestly believe, meet again, this time without your meddling family to try and force a wedge between us.'

You'll meet in hell with any luck, thought Lawrence Beauregard who had never liked his aunt and delighted in the infirmity that left her confined to the Long Island estate. He thought the reading a ridiculous sham. If only she knew what he knew about the dear departed patriarch. While he hadn't actually seen the old man at some of the night spots, he sometimes frequented himself, he knew the girls at these establishments who had met him.

'This concludes the reading of the last will and testament of Hamilton Monk. There remains only one item left. He desired upon the conclusion of the reading that all should rise and offer a toast to his memory. You will see before you that Froome has kindly provided a small glass of sherry for us.'

There was a moment of embarrassed silence, then Jefferson, followed by Quincy, rose from the table, which caused a chain reaction around the table. Soon everyone was on their feet, glass in hand, staring up at the portrait.

Belmont cleared his throat, once more, and raised his glass.

'To Hamilton Monk.'

And everyone in the room dutifully repeated the toast, except Froome. His eyes scanned the faces of the family members around the table. He felt his insides knot in anger at the naked hypocrisy on display.

He felt very angry indeed.

5

As Bobbie was drinking her tea, the door opened suddenly. Bobbie's head snapped around, expecting to see one of the late banker's sons appear. Instead, she found herself looking at a woman peaking her head around the corner of the door. The woman was in her mid-thirties and elegantly attractive, with a neat bob for her fair hair. She might well have been a model for Nell Brinkley.

'Oh, I'm sorry,' said the woman. 'I was looking for a couple of children. Sorry, may I ask who you are waiting for?'

Bobbie smiled and replied, 'I'm Roberta Flynn. I was asked by my...editor,' this sounded better than the head of obituaries, 'to visit the house and interview Mr Monk. This was at the request of Mr Monk who wanted to speak about his late father.' The woman nodded as if in recognition. Then Bobbie added, 'when I arrived fifteen minutes ago, I saw two young girls pass me at the gate.'

'Where were they headed?'

'Towards the park,' replied Bobbie with a frown. 'Is everything ok?'

The woman waved her hand airily, 'I'm sure it is. They're always running off without telling anyone where they go. Have they not finished the meeting?'

Bobbie shrugged, 'I'm not sure. I saw Mr Froome, but he said to wait here for Mr Monk.'

'The family must be chewing over the will,' said the woman. She walked into the room and shook the hand of Bobbie, who rose to her feet. 'I'm Olivia Belmont. My husband is the family lawyer.'

'You must have known Mr Monk very well. I'm sorry for your loss.'

Mrs Belmont looked remarkably sanguine about the loss of the banker but tried, for appearances sake, to demonstrate some latent grief.

'Oh, it was terrible, such a loss,' she breathed.

'A surprise too I imagine,' prompted Bobbie.

'Yes. He never gave any impression that he was suffering. But then the suicide note showed how he must have been really feeling.'

'Indeed,' replied Bobbie, who had not been aware of a suicide note. She said nothing, hoping it might create a vacuum that Mrs Belmont would feel the need to fill. She did.

'I guess he couldn't take seeing Mrs Monks' illness anymore. It's so, so tough for everyone.'

'Her illness?' asked Bobbie innocently. She was aware that she was perilously close to pushing her luck. However, the fact that she'd helped with setting a mother's mind at peace with the news of the children perhaps weighed in her favour.

Mrs Belmont pointed to her head, 'It's been a couple of years now. It's been getting worse lately. I'm not sure she even knew him at the end. He said that in the letter.'

'I'm so sorry,' replied Bobbie, and gave a silent prayer of thanks that her own father was a picture of health, both physically and mentally. Too much so. She still found it difficult to keep up with him when they walked on the street. What was it with men? Always needing to get somewhere quickly. Did they even know why they were rushing? She would never understand them.

A noise, outside in the corridor, disturbed the two women. They turned to the door and then back to one another.

'It sounds like they're finished. I'll leave you to it.'

'I'm sure your daughters are OK,' smiled Bobbie.

'Daughter,' replied Mrs Belmont. 'Violet is with Lydia, Jefferson, and Teddy's daughter.

Bobbie was surprised by this and said, 'They're very alike. I took them for sisters.'

Mrs Belmont laughed at this, 'Yes, many people do. They're great friends, almost as if they had known each other all their lives.'

'It was nice to meet you,' said Mrs Belmont. At this, she turned and walked to the door of the drawing room. When she reached it, she again turned and said, 'For what it's worth, I liked the old man. Spoke his mind. Didn't suffer fools. Maybe that upset a few people, but he was always decent with me. I can't say that about everybody. I hope you'll be kind to him.'

Bobbie grinned supportively but made no commitment.

Mrs Belmont left the room. Bobbie sat down and tried to listen to what was being said outside the room. She could hear Mrs Belmont speaking to someone in the corridor, but it was too difficult to make out what was being said.

Moments later, the door opened, and a man walked in. He looked like Rudolf Valentino's better-looking brother. His dark hair was a little dishevelled and he had more than a mere trace of five o'clock shadow, but his blue eyes had a hint of the devil and they crinkled nicely when he smiled at Bobbie.

'You really are, aren't you?' said the man by way of introduction.

'I really am Roberta Flynn from the *New York American* if that's what you mean,' replied Bobbie stiffly. Male attention was something she was used to by now. It was not necessarily unwelcome, but she disliked it when the flattery came basted in dismissive arrogance. Yet was this really worse than fearfulness with the opposite sex?

'Not quite, Miss Flynn. The *New York American* you say?'

'Yes, Mr Monk's son requested that we do a piece on the late Mr Monk. Something more than an obituary.'

'Ahh,' said the man, who leaned against the door and smiled lazily. It is a truth universally acknowledged by women that the most attractive smiles are lazy and dangerous, rather than earnest and good humoured. This man's smile was all of those things and more. No wonder women make such fools of themselves, thought Bobbie as she rose from her seat.

'Are you Mr Monk?' she asked hoping that the answer was yes and no. Both would be equally acceptable.

'I am,' confirmed the young man, looking Bobbie up and down and making no secret of the fact that he liked what he saw. 'But not the one you want. I am Quincy. I think it's my brother, Jefferson, who wishes to speak with you, as I don't remember asking to see a newspaper. If I'd known they would send a reporter like you, I might have been a bit more active. Jefferson's the head of the family now. The head of the bank. The old head on young shoulders.'

'And you?'

'Your servant,' said Quincy, bowing ostentatiously, before standing back to allow the door to open.

A man walked in, who looked like Quincy only a little bit older and less good-looking. They didn't so much look like brothers as two halves of the same coin. One was mature, responsible and serious. The other was young, disreputable and charming.

Jefferson Monk stared at his brother for a moment and then regarded Bobbie carefully.

'You are from the newspaper?'

'I am,' confirmed Bobbie. 'Roberta Flynn.' She walked forward with her hand outstretched. 'Please accept my commiserations for your loss.'

The elder Monk shook hands with Bobbie and nodded in reply to her comment.

'I'm sorry about being so late, I had forgotten we had a meeting today.'

'Would you like me to come back at another time?' asked Bobbie, hoping that she could get this over with as soon as possible. She was desperately curious to know how her article was being received back at the offices.

'No, I have time now. Well, an hour anyway. Will that be sufficient?'

'Yes, that would be great,' replied Bobbie. She turned and went back to her seat, while Jefferson sat opposite her. She did not take notice of Quincy leaving the room.

'Let's get started,' said Monk. His tone was not unfriendly, but it was business-like, which made Bobbie feel more comfortable. The thought of verbal jousting, with this man's brother, was not what she wanted when she was trying to work.

'What do you want to know?' asked Monk.

What do you want us to know wondered Bobbie.

6

Central Park, New York; 2nd January 1922

Bugsy McDaid was just minutes away from the worst twenty-four hours of his life. It was a life, it must be said, that had been notable only for its singular lack of achievement, education, or any accomplishment that Bugsy could lay claim to. He was half Irish and half Spanish and enjoyed none of the best features of either race. He had his father's red hair and pale skin while his mother had bequeathed him her volcanic temper and a level of patience that could be timed by the second. And that was when things were going well.

So far, the day had not turned, as so many had, against him; Nemesis was standing ready chuckling happily to himself.

Bugsy was a small man in every way, which contrasted markedly with his view of himself.

Standing with Bugsy was a man who was under no illusions about himself or the man he was with. Renat Murdrych had grown up in the harsh, cold climate of Russia, in a small town called Vorkuta. The town was so close to the Arctic Circle that he was virtually a polar bear. He was certainly as big as one and Bugsy, who was fond of a flutter at the track, would have given good odds that he'd beat one in a street fight.

Renat had escaped from one of the first gulags in Siberia created by the communist government in the newly formed Soviet Union and made his way across the Bering Sea to Alaska and eventually arrived in New York, five months after his original flight. During the civil war, between the whites and the reds, he'd chosen the wrong side. Upon capture, he had taken the name of a prominent intellectual, who had perished alongside him in the fight. This mistake could easily have been spotted after only a few moments conversation with the big Russian. However, his captors were no more educated than he was. They believed his silence was a sign of his intelligence. Like many intellectuals, he ended up in Siberia.

By the time the Soviet guards at the Gulag realised the mistake they already had the six-foot six strongman working on a railroad in the snow. His seeming imperviousness to the cold made him an asset in this rather challenging environment.

The two men sat in Central Park, on a day that was icy enough for Bugsy to feel his eyeballs freezing over. He had been complaining, ceaselessly, all morning in fact. Renat said nothing, as usual. He had never been the talkative kind, even in his homeland. He merely wondered what the problem was. January in New York seemed altogether pleasant to him.

They sat watching two little girls play. Both wore white dresses. Both had fair hair with a ribbon. They might have been twins. Bugsy was complaining about this too.

'I mean couldn't one of them have worn a different dress? How difficult can it be?' grumbled Bugsy. His face disappeared behind a vapour as he spoke. He shook his head and rose to his feet and shouted a few words to the skies, which would not have found favour at Sunday School. Bugsy did this from time to time when it seemed, as it often did, that the fates were stacked against him. His pale features turned scarlet on these occasions. Renat found it all rather amusing. The first words he had learned in English, inevitably, had been swear words. Over the two years he had been in the country his understanding of the language had improved markedly. but he would never sound like Oscar Wilde.

Renat nodded and stared at the two children. A thought occurred to him.

'Take both?' suggested the big Russian.

'No,' snapped Bugsy. 'Just the banker's daughter. That's where the money is.' He stamped his feet as he felt the cold bite through the paper-thin leather of his shoes.

Renat shrugged. One, both, it was all the same to him. He looked at the man with him. He could not quite bring himself to think of Bugsy as a comrade. Bugsy would decide what they did. This was always the way with Renat. He felt more comfortable taking orders.

'Well, we're going to have to pick one of them,' whined Bugsy. He smacked his fist into his hand and stared at the two girls who were playing chase just fifty yards in front of them.

Just then fate, that fickle comedian, made the decision for the two men and on this hung the series of misfortunes that befell them.

The snow lay thick and cold on the ground of Central Park. Neither girl cared. It was heaven for them. Lydia Monk ducked a flying snowball and laughed triumphantly. The next one hit her body a split second later. Typical Violet. There was always a trick up her sleeve. This made her laugh, even louder, at getting caught out like this.

Moments later her laughter turned to fear. She heard a dog barking. Not just barking. It was snarling. Nearby.

She turned and saw where the sound was coming from. Lydia had a fear of dogs. On the lead they were just about acceptable. Off the lead and she became terrified. This one was off the lead, and it was running right at her.

Don't be so scared they would say. They're friendly. Lydia was not so convinced. Right at that moment the only thing she knew was that this dog meant her harm and she was terrified.

Violet Belmont saw what was about to happen. Don't scream she thought. Don't scream, Lydia.

Lydia screamed.

The dog's barks seemed to Lydia to be directed at her. It's intent all too clear. Somewhere in the distance an owner shouted at *her*. 'Don't scream'.

Lydia screamed again.

She screamed so loud it woke an old tramp, snoozing against a tree, a bottle in his hand.

She screamed so loudly that the dog was now a hunter.

Lydia stared at the dog as it drew nearer and nearer, with unstoppable speed. The screaming had stopped. She was now mute with fear. Then all of a sudden, the dog stopped dead in its tracks and yelped.

A snowball had caught it in the body. It stopped in utter confusion and looked around. That was its big mistake. The next snowball caught it flush on the nose. The freezing snow stung the mutt. And scared it too. Violet Belmont gathered up the next snowball and clipped the ear of the retreating dog with her next throw. She had an unerring precision with snowballs.

'How dare you do that,' shouted the owner, still fifty yards away.

Violet turned to the owner and poured a volley of invective in his direction, which would have made a docker blush. She ran over to her friend, who had collapsed onto the wet snow, crying. She grabbed the outstretched hand of her friend and yanked her up and then proceeded to scold her.

'Look at your dress, silly,' said Violet Belmont. She pointed to a long, wet patch stained vaguely by green on Lydia's skirt. 'You won't get the blame for this either, I will.' Then she hugged her friend because there was nothing else she could think to do.

Lydia was caught between the terror of the attack and being amused by her friend scolding her. She began to laugh. Violet's cries that it was not funny made her laugh all the harder. Soon, even Violet's censure was somewhat undermined by the fact that she was laughing too. They composed themselves and thought of what to do next.

'We should go back,' said Violet. Her friend was shaking a little and it was more than just the cold.

'No,' said Lydia firmly. She'd already caused enough of a panic. She just wanted to play now. She scanned the park to make sure the dog was long gone and then she spotted a patch of bushes and trees. This presented an idea to her.

'What about hide and seek?'

Violet was less sure. She frowned. This was met with Lydia's hands going on her hips. This was a universal sign that a young lady's mind was made up. Violet relented, albeit reluctantly.

'Rules?' asked Violet.

The two girls had learned the hard way before that Violet's ingenious ability to hide had caused one or two incidents that wreaked havoc in the household, as they had searched for the missing child. Both mothers had insisted that they set a time limit of not more than five minutes when hiding, to avoid any future repetition.

'Five minutes,' said Lydia. 'You can hide first, and I'll count to fifty.'

'Fifty?' repeated Violet, as she did a quick survey of the terrain. She deliberately looked in the direction that she fully intended avoiding. This was an old trick of hers that Lydia had not yet cottoned on to.

'Hands,' said Violet which prompted Lydia to grin, then dutifully put her hands up to her eyes. As she did this, the count began.

'Fifty, forty-nine, forty-eight...'

Violet shot off in the direction she had been looking, another old trick but about twenty yards away from her best friend, she diverted sharply and sprinted towards a bush near the benches. She passed two men and put her fingers to her lips, in the universal sign of "don't say anything". The two men looked at one another and smiled then the smaller one nodded.

Violet ducked behind the bush, her heart racing, and waited. One of the men that she had seen on the seat, the one who had nodded, walked past her but did not look in her direction. He walked to an exit which was about thirty yards behind her. Violet, for wont of anything else to do, watched him walk through the exit and step into the driver's seat of a car.

One person fewer to give the game away, thought Violet. She kept her eyes on the man who seemed happy to stay in the car. Probably waiting for his friend, she concluded. The count almost certainly would have finished, and she heard in the distance confirmation of this as Lydia shouted, 'Here I come, ready or not.'

Violet's heart was beating fast. She loved this game. The chance to exercise her mind, and mischief against her best friend. She risked a glance from the side of the bush to see if her ruse had worked.

It had. Lydia tore off in the direction of the big American Sycamore tree that had caught her eye. It had an enormous grey-brown trunk that could hide a Lacrosse team.

As she was looking at Lydia sprint towards the tree, Violet heard the crunch of footsteps behind her. She turned and looked up. What she saw did not bode well.

It did not bode well at all.

7

While Jefferson Monk may not have had his brother's devil-may-care good looks, there was something oddly compelling about him. He radiated a ferocious combination of intelligence and energy. In Bobbie's view, this man was born to lead. Whether that was for good or for ill, she had not yet determined.

Monk was sitting in front of her now. His posture was erect, his collar starched to within an inch of its life and he wore a blue bow tie, with white polka dots. He looked to be around forty, but dressed like he was sixty years of age. Maybe it was something bankers felt they had to do – convey timeless timelessness. Bobbie suspected he was probably younger than forty, but responsibility and overwhelming ambition add years to a man, in many ways.

'What do you want to know?' he'd asked, and it was time to start the interview.

'Tell me a little about how your father came to start a bank. He was not born into money,' said Bobbie.

This brought a half-smile from Jefferson, He said 'Like me?'

Bobbie coloured a little, but smiled back and answered politely, 'Yes, like you.'

Monk provided a detailed answer to Bobbie's question that was genuinely fascinating. The life of Hamilton Monk had been almost Dickensian in the challenges he'd faced. He'd grown up near the border between what became battle lines for the north and the south, a few years before the start of the Civil War. It was a rich family, impoverished by the war. All the while as Monk spoke, Bobbie wondered why a man, who had faced such hardship in his life, would suddenly cave in, as he saw his wife's mind slowly disintegrate with age. Yes, it was probably heart-breaking, but the man Monk had described struck her as someone who would want to be with her through it all.

This made Bobbie curious and she probed more about the relationship between Hamilton Monk and his wife, Jefferson Monk's mother. The banker became visibly moved as he described the struggles they'd faced in having children. Jefferson Monk, the first born, had arrived around ten years after they had married with Quincy following five years later. It further confirmed the impression in Bobbie that the police may have been too quick to take his death at face value.

Towards the end of the interview, Bobbie asked the question uppermost in her mind, as she's listened to the banker.

'Mr Monk, having heard you describe your father, I am astonished that such a man would have taken his own life. He strikes me as a fighter.' Monk's eyes widened upon hearing this. He stared at Bobbie for a moment, and she wondered if she'd given offence. 'I'm sorry...' she began.

'No,' interrupted Monk. 'No, don't apologise Miss Flynn. I don't think that he was a man to have committed suicide either. Yet, how to explain the suicide note? It...'

He stopped for a moment and became, for the first time, emotional. He shook his head, perplexed. Before Bobbie could point out that suicide notes could be faked, there was an urgent knocking at the door. Moments later, Teddy Monk burst into the room. There were tears in her eyes. She shifted her glance from Jefferson to Bobbie and then back to her husband.

'Jefferson, you need to come now. Something's happened.'

The banker rose to his feet immediately, muttered an 'Excuse me,' and went straight to his wife. His wife glanced at Bobbie and then looked into her husband's eyes. She shook her head.

Monk turned to Bobbie and said, 'Perhaps you could talk to the staff, Miss Flynn. I think they could provide you with more information about my father. They loved him.'

Bobbie nodded and watched as the banker and his wife disappeared from the room. She was all alone now. Rather than stay seated she did what any sensible investigative reporter would have done. She rushed to the door and heard two words.

'...is missing.'

Bugsy McDaid looked at the young girl, slumped unconscious, in the back of the car. She was very pale. She was the golden goose. The last thing they needed was anything to happen to her. That was definitely not part of the plan.

'What did you do to her anyway?' snarled Bugsy from the driver's seat. 'If you've hurt her there'll be hell to pay.'

The big Russian, who was sitting in the back, was still feeling his way in the English language, but his partner's reaction to the condition of the young girl required no translation. He did what he usually did when confronted with the unknowable. He shrugged.

This was hardly guaranteed to reassure Bugsy and a stream of oath-laden invective went heading in the direction of Renat. He was used to this and could care less. Perhaps, when they made their fortune from this little escapade, then he might just supplement his income with that of his partner's.

The car was now on the other side of Third Avenue Bridge and very soon they arrived at their destination. The house was a small, two-bedroomed affair that looked as if it was minutes away from falling down. Bugsy and Renat shared the house with half a dozen rats, who wandered about with impunity, ignoring the traps that the Russian had laid down. They seemed to take it in turns to be chased by Renat. Bugsy had ceased to worry about them and seemed as amused as the rats were by the Russian's repeated failure to catch them.

But Renat had a plan to deal with this.

Bugsy pulled over and parked the car outside the house. He quickly scanned the street and saw that it was, mercifully, empty.

'I'll run over to the house and open the door. We'll need to get her in fast while no one is around.'

Renat had already worked that out for himself. He stepped outside the car and went around to the side of the car where the girl was slumped. Upon seeing Bugsy open the front door, he quickly picked up the child, like she was a rag doll and clumped over to the house.

By now, Violet was coming to, much to Bugsy's relief. She was still very groggy so had not yet quite worked out what was happening. However, she was also sharper than the flimflam man on Broadway and her mind was already clicking into action.

Renat landed through the front door, aimed a thirteen-inch boot at a couple of their rodent tenants, who swiftly evaded being sent into the Harlem River and almost landed on his back in the process. Bugsy let out a cackle at this, before collapsing into a cough that he refused to blame on the cigarettes that were a permanent feature in his mouth.

The front room had a sofa, rotting floorboards and smelled of boiled cabbage and mice. Violet hoped this wasn't what was on the menu. She closed her eyes as she did not want to alert the men who had, apparently abducted her, to the fact that she was awake.

Renat carried her through to the bedroom. As accommodation went, it was unlikely to challenge the Waldorf Astoria, in terms of comfort or desirability. A rusting metal bed, minus any sheets or, apparently, cotton stuffing in the mattress, dominated a room so desolate that even the paint appeared to be leaving.

'Be it ever so humble,' cracked Bugsy, but this was lost on Renat. The Russian laid the young girl gently on the bed. Her body shifted slightly on the mattress which brought a sign of relief from Bugsy. He genuinely had feared that his partner had overdone the chloroform.

'We'll let her sleep it off,' said Bugsy. 'Stay here in case she wakes.' With that, he left the room to make a coffee. For himself.

Fifteen minutes later, Renat appeared. He motioned for Bugsy to join him. Perhaps their captive was showing the first signs of life. Bugsy rose to his feet and ignored the Russian's glance towards the coffee cup.

The two men walked into the bedroom and stared down at the young girl who was now shifting around in the bed. She moaned a little and then, without warning, sat bolt upright. She stared at the two men and then her surroundings.

Her first words were not quite what Bugsy thought appropriate from a ten-year-old girl. In fact, this would not be the first time that Bugsy was to express dismay at the quality of parenting in 1922 and the discipline of kids "nowadays".

'Where the hell am I?' she said. Her voice was quite even and she seemed, at that moment, quite unafraid. Confused certainly, but, thankfully, free of any hysteria that Bugsy associated with women generally and young children, particularly.

'I don't want you to worry Miss Monk, but you have been kidnapped, by myself and my friend here. Once your Pa pays, up we'll release you and you can go back home.'

The young girl listened, with an unnerving lack of emotion, to this announcement. Then she leaned forward and said, in a worryingly even voice, her arm draped over her raised knees.

'And I don't want to worry you mister, but you got yourself the wrong girl.'

8

Bobbie's position at the door was proving an exquisitely painful combination of perfect for eavesdropping while being utterly vulnerable to any sudden entrance. From what she could gather from listening to the conversation in the hallways, one of the girls she had seen earlier had been kidnapped. Logically this had to be the daughter of Jefferson Monk.

And yet...

She listened more closely and heard the voice of the woman she'd met earlier, Olivia Belmont, she seemed to be crying and shouting. This made no sense to Bobbie so she continued to listen hoping that someone would shed light on the subject.

A voice was on the telephone, demanding that the police come immediately. Then, silence descended outside the door. Bobbie could hear the sound of footsteps echoing on the tiled floor. Someone had suggested launching a search of the park. Bobbie rushed to the window and saw the Monk brothers and some other men, including staff, running down the pathway and then turning in the direction of Central Park. Accompanying them was one of the young girls, that Bobbie had seen earlier.

When the coast was clear, Bobbie made for the door and exited the room to find the hallway empty. She looked around for some inspiration. The phone was awfully tempting. This would be a scoop. She rejected that option as soon as it entered her head. Her knowledge of townhouses was relatively hazy so she decided to go in the direction that she imagined might lead towards the kitchen.

This was not much of a plan but staying in the room seemed no better. Like most plans, it lasted barely seconds as she bumped into a woman.

'Who are you?' exclaimed the woman in shock at seeing a stranger. Then her eyes narrowed, and she said, 'Are you the reporter that Jefferson was meeting earlier?'

'Yes,' confirmed Bobbie. 'My name is Bobbie Flynn. I'm from the *New York American*.' This brought a frown from the woman. Bobbie realised her continued presence in the house hung by a thread, if the woman's facial expression was anything to go by. Just as the woman was about to execute the *coup de grace*, Bobbie added quickly, 'I'm sorry but I couldn't help but overhear. Has your daughter been kidnapped?'

The woman was taken aback by the directness, as well as the perspicacity, of the young woman she was facing. It created a dilemma, one that Bobbie had fully intended it should, on whether she confirm or deny and then face the prospect of a reporter running to the offices to report on what had happened. This would not do.

As Teddy Monk was weighing up what to do, Bobbie played her ace. Or to be more exact, her aces.

'Look, Mrs Monk, I understand the last thing you need right now is to have a reporter here in the house. I give you my word that if you ask me to leave, I will not say anything to my editor. The last thing I would ever do is put your daughter's life in any danger. I really hope that this is not the case, by the way and that they find her.'

Teddy Monk's eyes welled up with tears, but she was oddly composed given the horrible circumstances.

'I believe that I might be able to help you,' added Bobbie, playing her final ace.

The frown reappeared on Teddy's face. It was a mixture of confusion and irritation, which made Bobbie realise that she had to tread carefully.

'My father is a senior policeman with the NYPD. His name is Inspector Flynn. I'm sure I could prevail upon him to come here and handle this matter personally.'

Teddy Monk's eyes widened in shock at this, then narrowed again.

'You better not be lying to me.'

'I'm not. Ring the NYPD and ask to be put through to Inspector Flynn.'

For a few moments, Teddy stared at Bobbie and then, finally, relented. She marched over to the telephone and lifted the receiver to her ear and spoke into the mouthpiece.

'Hello, can you put me through to the NYPD. This is an emergency.'

A few moments later she was requesting that she be put through to Inspector Flynn. It took a minute of waiting then a voice came through on the receiver that Bobbie knew all too well.

'Inspector Flynn, who is speaking?"

Teddy handed the phone to Bobbie.

'Hello daddy, it's Bobbie.'

'What do you want, Bobbie? I have an emergency here,' shouted Flynn.

Bobbie glanced at Teddy who nodded back to her.

'Daddy, that's why I'm calling you. I'm in the Monk house right now. It doesn't matter why I'm here, but the Monk child may have been kidnapped. I'm with Mrs Monk right now.'

Teddy Monk took the phone away from Bobbie and spoke into the mouthpiece once more, 'Hello, Inspector Flynn. This is Theodora Monk. I'm with your daughter. Is there someone coming over? We are very concerned. There's one other thing you should know...'

Just then there was a rap at the door. Instinctively, Bobbie went to answer it as she was only a few feet away. She opened the door and found herself staring at a young policeman she had met only a few days previously.

'Detective Nolan,' exclaimed Bobbie.

'Miss Flynn,' replied Nolan with a good deal less enthusiasm which Bobbie noted. The detective in question, Nolan, was six-foot, half Irish, half Italian with dark wavy hair and blue eyes. 'What are you doing here?'

There was no point in asking Nolan the same question, so she stood back and allowed the detective, along with a patrolman that she did not know, to step into the house.

Teddy Monk was just putting the phone down.

'Mrs Monk, may I introduce Detective Nolan. He and my father recently worked together on a murder case. They were instrumental in helping prevent another death.'

'So were you,' murmured Nolan, glancing towards Bobbie. Then he returned his gaze to Teddy Monk. Striding forward, he shook Teddy Monk's outstretched hand. Even she found herself temporarily muted by the tall, good-looking detective. Then she collected herself. In another room, they could hear someone crying and all eyes went to the door. It was a woman and she was near hysteria.

'Mrs Monk, I gather your daughter is missing,' said Nolan.

'Not quite Detective Nolan. It's not my daughter who's missing. It's Violet Belmont. That's her... mother crying,' replied Teddy, flicking her eyes towards the door and missing the look of shock on Bobbie's face. Both Bobbie and Nolan noted the slight pause as she had spoken.

'I should go to see her,' said Nolan. 'May I?'

'Of course,' replied Teddy.

Bobbie decided that she could follow them and they went towards the room from where the sound of crying was coming.

At that moment the phone rang. Its shrill tine sounded like an alarm in the middle of the night. All eyes turned to the phone. Nolan motioned for Teddy to pick the phone up, but he joined her near the earpiece.

A voice she did not recognise came on the line.

'Mrs Monk, we have your daughter. If you want to see her alive again, you'll do exactly as we say.'

Then the line went dead.

9

'I'm not her daughter you big ape,' screamed Violet from behind the door of her room.

It was the first time that anyone had ever called Bugsy big and he might have considered basking in the glow of the moment, but to be described as an ape was taking things just too far. Rage poured through him and he burst into the room where the young girl was being held.

'Look kid I've had just about all I can take from you. I don't know what your parents are doing, but you're the worst behaved brat I've ever met and I've met quite a few,' snarled Bugsy, his face inches away from Violet's, his finger jabbing her chest painfully.

Violet Belmont had something of a reputation of being badly behaved and she was rather proud of this. One of the reasons for this bad behaviour, her parents believed, and with some justification, was the fact that she was unusually precocious. Violet was, by quite some distance, the brightest child in her class at the private school she attended. Such praise could not and had not, ever been levelled at Bugsy McDaid. What Bugsy had said was laughably hypocritical. Violet, who was part of a lawyer's household, realised she was dealing with a card-carrying idiot.

'What are my parents doing?' said Violet, slowly with a half-smile. 'What about yours? Their kid grew up a child kidnapper.'

The sound of the wind evaporating from the sails of Bugsy was like a clap of thunder. First Bugsy's eyes widened and then so too did Violet as she realised, not for the first time, that she may have taken things a little too far.

Bugsy lifted her up and was seconds away from hurling her onto the bed when he felt a restraining arm from Renat.

'No,' said the talkative Russian.

Bugsy put her down again and stalked out of the room. This left Renat with a little girl who was breathing very heavily. Scared, but unbowed, she glared up at Renat. Renat bent down and put his face near hers. He lifted a finger and pointed it between her eyes.

'No,' he said before turning and walking out of the room. He slammed the door shut. Violet stared at the door and listened as she heard the sound of a key turning in the lock. Out of the sight of the two men, she sloped over to the bed and buried her head in the mattress. Free to give vent to her emotions, she did so. Her body shook with the violence of her sobs. It lasted a few minutes and then she sat up on the bed.

Enough.

They were going to make her life hell.

Well, she could play at that game, too.

The men from the Monk household returned fifteen minutes later accompanied by half a dozen policemen. They were surprised to see the hallway empty.

'Where is everyone?' said Monk as he strode into his house.

He went over to the dining room where, earlier, the will had been read. It was then he heard the sound of voices. Opening the door he found his wife with Olivia Belmont as well as the young woman who had interviewed him earlier. There were two men, both policemen.

Detective Nolan, who had been perched on the dining table, stood up and walked towards the new arrivals who were piling into the room.

'I'm Detective Nolan, may I ask which of you is Mr Belmont?'

Fitzroy Belmont stepped forward. There was trepidation in his voice.

'I am Belmont, Detective Nolan.'

'Sir, I'm sorry to confirm this, but your daughter has been kidnapped. We received a phone call while you were out conducting a search. We believe this is a case of mistaken identity. The kidnappers believe they have Lydia Monk.'

'What do they want?' demanded Jefferson Monk.

Nolan turned to Monk with a slight frown. He was not so dull-witted not to recognise that this was probably Jefferson Monk, but the manner in which he usurped the father's moment of shock had irritated him. Nolan stared at Monk and waited for him to introduce himself.

'I'm Jefferson Monk. It's my daughter they were after.'

Nolan nodded at this and then replied, 'The call came a few minutes ago. They did not say anything about what they want, but a ransom demand will be on its way, either by mail or they will call us.'

'So, what do we do?' asked Belmont, trying to contain his emotions.

Nolan sighed before answering, 'I'm afraid all we can do is wait for the call. In the meantime, I will send men out to see if there were any witnesses to the abduction. The park is usually full of people. Someone must have seen something.'

Jefferson Monk had not become the head of a bank by sitting around and waiting for something to happen. By birth, by education and by personality he was a man of action. The idea that they should just sit around and wait for the kidnappers to dictate terms was antithetical to everything that made him who he was. He wanted to slam his fist on the table, he certainly would have had they been in a boardroom, but he had to make do with the palm of his other hand.

'That's not good enough,' he shouted. 'We can't just sit here on our hands and wait.'

'We are not,' pointed out Nolan, calmly. 'I instructed the men, when the search finished, to split up. Some to go door-to-door to find out if anyone saw anything. The other half were to go around the park and speak to people there to find any eyewitnesses. At the precinct, before I left, I had a man check up on known kidnappers who have been released from prison in the last year. Each one will get a visit from a patrolman. We also have a man checking on hotels and motels in the city and beyond. Aside from that sir, if you have any better suggestions then I am prepared to listen.'

The two men faced off. The banker reddened slightly; his mouth curled into an angry snarl. It wasn't helped by the fact that he could see his brother, with a half-smile on his face. Jefferson Monk was not used to people speaking back to him. Worse, he was not used to people pointing out the obvious flaws in what he had said. Silence fell on the room. The only noise came from some voices in the corridor.

'I want to see your commanding officer young man,' said Monk finally.

'That would be me,' said a voice in the doorway.

All eyes turned towards the man who had just arrived.

Inspector Flynn stepped forward. He was a man in his late fifties, with a full head of grey hair and eyes that had seen a lot of life, death and everything in between.

'Who are you?' asked Monk. His tone was a little more considered as he recognised a man that would not be easily bullied. To be fair, the young detective appeared to be made from similarly unyielding material.

'My name is Flynn,' said the detective. 'Inspector Flynn.'

He scanned the room, his eyes fixed first on Olivia Belmont. He didn't have to ask who she was. On one side of her was an attractive woman who was of a similar age to the banker. He guessed this was Mrs Monk. On the other side was his daughter.

'Hello Bobbie,' he said without the usual attendant enthusiasm a father should show for his daughter. Her desire to be an investigative reporter specialising in crime was a sore point between the two of them. He would have preferred her reporting to be confined to the millinery trade and its latest fashions. In this he was resigned to defeat, but he would continue to disapprove of her ambitions, nonetheless and fight the good fight.

Monk frowned when Flynn acknowledged Bobbie.

'You know this young woman?' asked the banker.

'My daughter,' said Flynn, unable to hide the sigh in his voice.

'Jefferson,' interjected Teddy Monk, 'It's thanks to this young woman that we have the inspector here. Miss Flynn called and asked for him specially.'

This was becoming a little bit overwhelming for the banker, but he had not become head of a bank for nothing. He was very quick on the uptake. He nodded to Bobbie and said in a mollified voice, 'Very well, I welcome you Inspector Flynn and thank you Miss Flynn for your help. Now, please will you tell me what you are going to do to get this young girl back. Fitzroy and Olivia, in fact all of us are out of our minds with worry.'

Flynn shot a look over to Nolan.

'What have you said?'

Nolan told him.

Then Flynn turned to Jefferson, while indicating with his thumb the young detective.

'Sadly, it's just what he said. There's nothing we can do until we either hear from the kidnappers or one of the patrolmen find a witness. I brought a few more men in on this so we have ten in all going door-to-door or in the park.' Then Flynn turned to Nolan once more and asked, 'Who have you checking the records?'

'Brains,' replied Nolan.

'Hotels and motels in the area?'

'Harrigan,' replied Nolan.

This was greeted with a grunt from Flynn, which Nolan and the rest of the room took to be approval. There was something about the craggy countenance of Flynn that appeared to appease the banker and provide reassurance. Any further desire to fight had evaporated and been replaced by a resigned acceptance, that everything that could be done was in play.

'OK,' continued Flynn, 'Nolan, I want you to speak to the staff and find out if anyone has seen any men near the house in the last few days. It's a long shot, but maybe someone has seen something. I'd like to speak to you Mr Monk and you Mrs Monk to know the names of everyone who has visited the house too. We need to speak to them in case they have anything that might help us.'

Teddy Monk nodded at this.

'Is there anything else we can do to help,' she asked.

Flynn thought for a moment and then replied, 'Well, a coffee would be a good start.'

10

Just before the coffee arrived, Flynn took his daughter into the corridor, to find out why she happened to be here, at the scene of yet another crime. They had both recently attended a New Year's party that resulted in a murder.* He was not happy and had never been a man to hide dismay, especially when dealing with a daughter, who had a low threshold when it came to disobeying her father.

Bobbie explained how she had only found out that morning about her assignment. Flynn was in no position to dispute the story but did so anyway as a matter of form.

'Seems awfully convenient to me, young lady,' he snapped.

Bobbie grinned at her father who clearly hadn't a leg to stand on, 'You should use me in the force Dad. This ability of mine to foretell a crime could be a real boon for the city's crime prevention.'

'That's enough from you,' said Flynn. He fixed his eyes on her and said, 'I don't want you getting involved with this, do you hear?'

'Shall I go back to the office, then?'

This point had been swilling around Flynn's mind too and the simple answer, he realised, was that there were no right answers. He could send her on her way and risk that she would let slip about the kidnapping before she was supposed to. This was a low risk as he trusted his daughter, up to a point. But she was ambitious and who knows what she might do? On the other hand, he could keep an eye on her in the house, but he knew her all too well. She would slowly insinuate herself into the investigation. He felt like howling to the moon. So, he did what he always did and sent her to her room. In this case it was the drawing room.

'OK young lady, I want you to sit in that room over there and don't move while I deal with this. Do you understand?'

'Yes, Dad,' smiled Bobbie. Nothing in her countenance gave the old detective any confidence that she would obey so much as a syllable of his request. Dutifully, she went to the drawing room and sat down. Her notebook was sitting on the table. Rather than let the time go to waste, she began to jot down her thoughts, on both the death of Hamilton Monk and the kidnapping.

Nothing about the death of the elder banker added up to her. There should, at least, have been more of an investigation. It made her wonder who had handled the case. It certainly wasn't her father, as he'd never mentioned it to her in the brownstone house they shared near Greenwich Village. Her mother had died a couple of years previously, leaving both her and Flynn bereft. She had adored her mother and took after her in many ways, but the analytical mind and the colouring of her hair made her very much her father's daughter.

Bobbie created two columns and jotted down thoughts as they occurred to her.

<u>*Hamilton Monk's Death*</u>.   <u>*Violet Belmont kidnapping*</u>

If it was murder, who benefitted?   Is it a mistake or was Violet the target?

Is it connected to kidnapping?   Is kidnapping connected to the will?

If so, is someone inside the house. Someone from house or unknown?

Responsible for both?

Bobbie's sense of frustration grew, as she thought about the two events. She was aware enough of her own foibles to accept that she might be correlating two things, that perhaps had no connection, because she wanted there to be one. She knew she had to guard against jumping to such conclusions. In this regard, she was following her father's advice although he had taught her this when she was at school working on science topics without any idea that she might one day use it in solving crimes.

It didn't help that she was stuck inside the drawing room, unable to do anything about either case. She heard a door opening and some footsteps in the corridor. Bobbie ran to the door and opened it a few inches. She saw Detective Nolan standing in the corridor looking around him, a little lost. Without thinking, she immediately stepped forward into the corridor to join him.

'Ah, there you are,' she said with a wide smile.

Nolan frowned when he saw her, which made him unusual as most men tended to smile stupidly. This was a point in his favour she supposed.

'What do you mean?' he asked.

'My father suggested I accompany you when you speak to the staff. He didn't want to say anything in front of Mr Monk, but he said to me it would be a good idea.'

'A good idea,' repeated Nolan, in the manner that most men do when they are not only sceptical of what they are hearing, but downright suspicious.

'Yes, I've already met some of the staff when I was interviewing them about the late Mr Monk. They know me and may be able to open up more about what has happened if I'm with you.'

'Really,' said Nolan. There was just enough uncertainty in his eyes to give Bobbie hope that she might yet get her way.

'I'll show you the way,' said Bobbie taking his arm and leading him towards the kitchen before he could marshal his forces to oppose her. The move took the detective by surprise and he found himself walking ahead, without having raised any serious objection to what was an obvious attempt to inveigle herself into the investigation.

A part of him was angry at his hopeless attempt at resistance, but this was mitigated by the realisation that he was dealing with the inspector's daughter. And, he had to admit, when they had last met a few days previously, she had proved to be quite resourceful. More worryingly was the undeniable fact that she was also quite beautiful.

Bobbie had no idea if she was actually leading Nolan to the kitchen, but it felt that she was heading in the right direction. She heard some voices further down a corridor and the clank of metal on metal which she took to be pots and pans. Sure enough they had managed to find the kitchen. Bobbie walked in praying that Froome would be there.

He was.

'Miss Flynn,' said Froome, rising from his chair. He patted his livery down to rid himself of the crumbs from the biscuit that he'd been eating. 'Are you lost?'

'No, far from it,' said Bobbie. She turned to Nolan who followed her into the kitchen. 'This is Detective Nolan. He wants to ask you all some questions about the disappearance of Violet. This is Mr Froome,' added Bobbie, indicating the aged butler.

There were two other people aside from Froome. One was a young woman who was a little younger than Bobbie, probably in her late teens. The older woman, clearly the cook, was in her thirties. The arrival of someone like Nolan prompted the two women to stand up straighter and smile at the handsome detective. Bobbie shot a glance towards Nolan who ignored her.

'As Miss Flynn says, I am Detective Nolan from midtown. You'll know now that Miss Violet has been abducted. We'll do all we can to find her. In the meantime, I need to ask you some questions.'

'Of course,' said Froome. 'Please take a seat. Eileen, Mary, please can you make a coffee for Detective Nolan and Miss Flynn.'

This was a very welcome idea. Froome took his seat, along with Bobbie and Nolan.

'Have you seen anyone in the area, hanging around the house over the last few days?' asked Nolan, taking out a notebook. This was met with a collective shake of the head. Nolan sighed at this and then asked, 'Have you had any deliveries this week? Anyone new that you haven't seen before?'

Again, more shakes of the head.

Bobbie cut in at this point, 'Did you spend Christmas here or at the Long Island house?'

Nolan glanced towards Bobbie and nodded. At least he wasn't one of those men who cannot accept that women have a mind, too, thought Bobbie.

'We spent the period between Christmas and New Year at the house in Long Island. There was little appetite for anyone to come into the city, to celebrate this year, as you may imagine.'

'So, this is the first day that you have been here since before Christmas?'

'Since that awful day when Mr Monk took his own life,' confirmed Froome, shaking his head sadly.

Which made it quite a coincidence, thought Bobbie, that the kidnappers chose today to try and abduct Lydia Monk. Bobbie, like her father, was suspicious of coincidences. She glanced towards Nolan. The detective appeared unhappy at what he'd heard. He didn't believe in coincidence either.

'It sounds like the kidnappers got very lucky,' said the detective before adding mordantly, 'until they took the wrong girl.'

11

More than ever, Bobbie was convinced that there was an element of suspicion surrounding the death of Hamilton Monk than the story the police had accepted so easily. It was time to reveal some of her hand. The coffee was now ready and while Eileen poured some into three cups, Bobbie decided to broach the subject once more with Froome.

'Mr Froome,' said Bobbie, 'Can you tell us more about the death of Mr Monk?'

Froome seemed surprised by the change in tack and certainly unsure about what it had to do with the abduction.

'Well, I'm not sure what else there is to say. What would you like to know?'

'Where did Mr Monk take his own life?' asked Bobbie.

Froome glanced towards the window and then said, 'It was in the summer house in the garden. We were all in the kitchen when we heard a gunshot. I advised Eileen and Mary to stay inside, while I went to investigate. I went outside and, when I reached the summer house, I found Mr Monk lying dead in his armchair. It was quite distressing.'

'I'm sure it was,' said Bobbie sympathetically. 'How long did it take you to reach the summer house after the gun shot?'

'Not very long, but I must confess, I did not rush. It was on my mind that there might be a madman in the garden with a gun. I looked from the kitchen first but did not see anyone. Then I asked Eileen to raise the alarm with the two Mr Monks while I went to investigate. All in all, I think it must have no more than two minutes before I found poor Mr Monk.'

'Were you the first to reach his body?'

'Yes, but his two sons arrived at the summer house less than a minute after me and then the ladies.'

Nolan remained silent all the while Bobbie was asking these questions. He frowned and looked at Bobbie. Unabashed, Bobbie pressed ahead.

'Who found the suicide note?'

'I'm not sure I remember. Was it Mrs Monk? Or perhaps the police? It was all a bit of a blur.'

'She went into the summer house?' asked Nolan, intrigued by the idea that the brothers had allowed anyone to see their dead father.

'It was rather difficult to stop Mrs Monk. I think you would need to see the summer house and you'll see what I mean.'

Bobbie was immediately on her feet. With a hopeful smile, she asked, 'Do you mind showing us, Mr Froome?'

Froome was still confused, but a lifetime of service blunts one's ability to question and amplifies the desire to do as one is told. He stood up, as did Nolan, who saw that he had no choice in the matter.

'Very well, if you will follow me, please.'

The old butler drained the rest of his coffee, as did Nolan and they moved towards the back door of the kitchen which led out to the garden.

The garden was relatively thin with a high wall at the back hidden behind English Ivy. At the end of the garden was a wooden summer house with a porch. There were French doors at the front of the summer house. As they neared the building, Bobbie could see that it was relatively small and that the interior would have been large enough for only a sofa and an armchair but, once the French doors were open, then the additional porch space meant that it would have comfortably accommodated ten people seated.

'Did Mr Monk normally spend time in the summer house, in the middle of winter?' asked Bobbie.

'No, it was rather unusual that he went out there. I imagine it was very cold and he quite detested the cold.'

Nolan was staring at Bobbie now, but she was unperturbed.

'You don't know if he was intending to meet someone there?' asked Bobbie.

'I'm afraid not. We did not realise he was out there, until we heard the gunshot.'

'How would he have accessed the garden?' asked Nolan, which made Bobbie grin in triumph. The detective seemed to be getting into the spirit of the inquiry, at last.

Bobbie resisted the temptation to shout, 'Attaboy, Nolan.'

'Through the French windows of the lounge,' replied Froome. He pointed over to the windows that led to a small patio area with steps down to the garden.

'There's no other way of reaching the summer house, other than through the lounge or the kitchen?'

'Correct, sir,' confirmed Froome.

Bobbie went up the steps and checked the door of the summer house. It was open. She walked inside. It was rather cold now and she regretted not bringing a coat. Vapour formed around her mouth as she breathed.

The room had obviously been thoroughly cleaned since the death of Monk as there was nothing to suggest anything untoward had happened there. Bobbie walked through the room to a door at the back wall, beside a bookcase and a large globe, which she presumed was a well-disguised cocktail cabinet. She resisted the temptation to verify this as she felt it would be a little unfair on their hosts to put them in a bad light in these Prohibition times.

The door, however, was too much of a temptation. She turned when she heard a creak on the wooden floorboards. It was Nolan and he was now standing rather close to her. She glanced up at him.

'What's on your mind Miss Flynn?' he asked. It is rather difficult to carry off a half-frown, half-smile, but the young detective managed it just at that moment and Bobbie couldn't decide if this was impressive, attractive, or both. She didn't want to think about it either, so she quickly turned to the door and opened it.

It was a toilet. Interestingly for Bobbie, there was a small window to the side which would allow someone, if they chose, to climb through. She glanced triumphantly at Nolan.

The detective shook his head and said, 'I sense you are racing ahead to a conclusion.'

'On the contrary Detective Nolan, you may not believe this, but it is possible for a woman to consider possibilities, without assuming that, by doing so, she has proved her case.'

'*Touché*,' said Nolan, but his face was impassive. He walked into the small bathroom and checked the window. It was bolted shut. From the inside. He turned to Bobbie and raised his eyebrows. It meant nothing of course as he well knew. The window *could* have been opened by an intruder beforehand.

'Can you unbolt it for me, please?' asked Bobbie.

With a roll of his eyes, Nolan did as Bobbie asked, then, they both walked back out of the small bathroom and through the summer house.

'And you don't know if Mr Monk met anyone in the summer house on the morning of his death?' asked Bobbie.

'No, Miss Flynn, I do not. I'm sorry,' answered Froome, genuinely sorry that he could not help.

They all returned to the garden. Bobbie immediately left the two men and walked around the side of the summer house to the window. It was a little bit high for her to climb through. She looked around to see if there was anything she could use to stand on. Separating the grass from the flower bed was a small log. Bobbie picked it up and set it down by the window. It gave her an eight-inch boost. Removing her shoes which had small heels on them and were a little bit of an inconvenience from a breaking and entering point of view, she stood on the log. The window opened easily.

Glancing around, she checked that the two men could not see her as her next action would certainly reveal a lot more of her than she felt comfortable with. Hitching up her skirt, to an indecently short, but highly practical length, she swung her leg up onto the sill. Then she pulled herself up and over, landing inside the bathroom in a bit of a heap. No matter, she had proven to her own satisfaction that it was possible with a little advance planning to gain entry to the summer house. Moments later, she came out onto the patio of the summer house, much to the evident surprise of Froome.

Bobbie smiled at Nolan and said, 'Someone could have come in through the bathroom window and escaped that way too.'

Nolan did not comment on this. Instead, he walked around the side and looked at the log by the window. In the background, he heard Bobbie call out to him to pick up her shoes. This made him smile, but he did as she asked and walked past the window to the area behind the summerhouse, where it met the wall covered with ivy. There was enough room for someone to hide there, which made him a little bit irritated. Was it possible that she was right?

He returned to the front of the summer house and handed the shoes to Bobbie who made a mock curtsey. Froome by this stage was aware of what was being implied by the young woman and the detective's subsequent actions.

'You're not suggesting that Mr Monk's death was murder, are you?' he asked with almost a palpable shake in his voice.

'I'm not,' said Nolan.

'I am,' said Bobbie at the same time.

'I think we should return to the house,' said Nolan and immediately marched off in the direction from which they had come. This left Bobbie and Froome with no alternative but to follow him.

Bobbie hopped along putting her shoe on then jogged up beside the detective.

'Go on, admit it,' she said smiling up at him.

'I will admit nothing,' said Nolan, feeling like a ten-year-old, caught with his hand in a cookie jar.

Bobbie did not believe this for one second and nor, she suspected, did Nolan. He had seen for himself that the investigating police had not done much by way of what their job description required.

Bobbie turned to Froome, who was having difficulty keeping up with the younger pair.

'Mr Froome, you are sure it was the police who found the suicide note?' asked Bobbie. She stopped to wait for the butler. So too did Nolan. This was an automatic reaction to Bobbie halting and he silently cursed himself for doing so. It implied interest in what the young woman was doing. Frustratingly for him, he realised she had a point.

'I believe it was the police who found it now that I think of it. They showed it to Mrs Monk who, I believe, confirmed the handwriting.'

'Not Mr Monk's sons?'

'No. I am certain that when the police came, they found the note. It had fallen to the floor and in all the confusion neither Mr Monk saw it lying there,' said Froome.

'Presumably, the detective showed the note to the sons, to confirm if it was Mr Monk's handwriting.'

'I understand that he did,' agreed Froome.

'Do you know what the note said?'

The butler shook his head. They were at the door of the kitchen. After wiping their feet, they walked inside and thanked Froome and the kitchen staff before heading back into the corridor. As they walked, they heard a commotion in the hallway. When they arrived there, they saw Flynn, Jefferson Monk and the two Belmonts standing by the phone.

Flynn turned to his daughter and Nolan; his eyes were lit with an angry fire.

'Where were you?' snapped Flynn.

Bobbie was about to respond when Nolan said, 'We wanted to check something in the garden.'

'You missed the call from the kidnappers,' responded Flynn irritably.

12

Bobbie followed her father and Nolan into the drawing room. It felt like they had been called into the headmaster's office and nothing on Flynn's face gave her any confidence that they were both about to receive anything other than an almighty ticking off.

The door shut behind them and then Flynn spun around. He was angry. Bobbie knew the signs and, even at twenty-one years of age, it still made her quail a little. She adored her father and had never once considered leaving the house they shared since the passing of her mother. The idea of him alone was too much for her to bear in that big brownstone. He rarely lost his temper, but when he did, it was as if the very foundations of any building trembled in the seismic rage. There was always a good reason and Bobbie suspected he had reason.

Flynn addressed himself to Nolan first.

'We are in the middle of a kidnap situation,' he said in a low, very intense whisper. 'It involves the life of a young girl. So, what on earth were you doing in the garden, with my daughter? What could possibly be more important than a young child's life?'

Put that way, the answer was clearly nothing.

However, Nolan was not someone to shrink from the fight, as his service during the war had shown. Nor had he become so well thought of in the ranks, and by senior officers, without having demonstrated a certain degree of initiative and intelligence. However, what he was about to say was likely to throw further fuel onto the flames.

'Sir, there is a possibility, and I repeat, it's only a possibility, but there may be a connection between the death of Hamilton Monk and the kidnapping.'

Bobbie held her breath, while she watched her father's face change from red hot rage to something less easy to interpret.

'Do you have a single shred of evidence that leads you to such a conclusion?'

This was said in an ice-cold whisper that chilled Bobbie. It was almost as if Nolan's career was now hanging by a thread and it was all her fault. She was the one who had led him outside. She was the one who had planted the seed of doubt in his mind, about the suicide of the banker. Now that seed was about to bear poisonous fruit.

'Not yet, sir,' said Nolan, in a voice that was as quietly angry as Flynn. Bobbie could see the fire burning in his eyes. 'And I don't believe I will be able to find any evidence of a connection if you or anyone else for that matter is not prepared to open their mind to the possibility that it exists.'

The defiant tone from the young man temporarily stopped Flynn in his tracks. He turned his attention to his daughter.

'Did you put these foolish thoughts in his head?' demanded Flynn.

While she may have been of Irish heritage and the proud possessor of red hair, generally Bobbie did not display the volatility so classically associated with those who combined such characteristics. This is not to say she did not know how to stage a volcanic eruption, when the occasion demanded. Sometimes this would be the result of molten lava flowing naturally, or sometimes it was for show. Most men cannot tell the difference anyway and will happily take cover, whatever the cause.

Bobbie could see that her father had a point, but it was time that she made hers. She stepped forward, feigned wide-eyed, nostril flaring anger and jabbed a finger at her father.

'Don't patronise me father and certainly not in front of your men. What if we are right?' hissed Bobbie at her father. She made sure to say 'we' which caused an eyebrow of Nolan not much to rise as shoot up like he'd been kicked in a sensitive area. 'What if there is a connection. You're the one that taught me not to believe in coincidence. Well, this is a pretty big coincidence in anyone's book. A suicide, a will reading and a kidnap?'

To be fair, it was and it had crossed Flynn's mind also. Still, it was never a good feeling to have thought something and said nothing, only to hear it played back to you by someone who now thinks you are narrow-minded, for not seeing what they can see.

As Bobbie had effectively "seen" and then raised the ante, Flynn now had a call to make, and he realised that his options were limited. He was saved, quite literally, by the bell. The doorbell to be precise. It rang giving the combatants time to back away to their corners even if round two was probably not too far away.

'Wait here,' snapped Flynn and he, along with Nolan, went to see who was at the door. Bobbie decided to do so. There are times when one must stand up and fight the good fight, there are others when one should head back to the clubhouse and have a gin and tonic. This, metaphorically, was one of those moments.

She heard her father's voice muffled behind the heavy door of the drawing room and then a few seconds later it opened. Her father walked in with Nolan, a patrolman and a man that dressed with all of the fashion sense of a scarecrow. His hair stuck up in a manner that suggested he had recently been subjected to electric shock treatment and his face had grime so deeply engrained it might have been tattooed there. When he saw Bobbie, he made a graceful bow and smiled shamelessly at her.

The next shock came when he spoke.

'Your servant, Miss,' said the tramp. Then he turned to Nolan as if he was a servant and said, 'I say, old chap, I don't suppose you have something to wet my lips. I'm somewhat parched. I don't mean water either. Ghastly stuff. Something stronger if you understand me.'

It was all too clear what he was asking for. Jefferson Monk appeared at the door and Flynn made a request that he never thought, as an officer of the law, he would ever or, indeed, should ever, ask.

'Have you any gin?'

Monk looked uncomfortable at this. These were Prohibition times after all and he was unsure of how it might go down if he was seen to be in possession of a stock of alcohol.

'Hurry man,' ordered Flynn. This sent Monk, a man not used to taking orders, scurrying off to find some alcohol.

Nolan and the patrolman led the man to a seat near Bobbie. Flynn was on the point of barking at his daughter to leave when she took matters into her own hand.

'You sound English, where are you from, sir?'

The man was obviously greatly taken with Bobbie. She judged him to be in his sixties and the refinement of his voice suggested someone who was either from the upper classes or had been a servant in such a household.

'I am English as you surmise. I hail from Surrey, a little town called Ascot.'

'Oh yes, I've heard of Ascot,' said Bobbie. 'They have horse racing there. Royal Ascot.'

'Very good miss,' replied the old tramp.

'And your name is?' asked Bobbie.

'Fogg, miss.'

'Fogg, may I ask you,' pressed Bobbie, 'Are you, or were you once, a servant in a big household.'

The old tramp's eyes widened, and he replied, 'My, miss, your perspicacity is quite exceptional. I can see why the noble members of the New York Police Department have brought women into their ranks.'

In fact, they hadn't, but Bobbie was not about to disabuse him of this notion, tempting as it was to make the point in front of her father and Nolan. However, just then Froome came in with a glass and bottle of gin. Froome glanced in the direction of Flynn who nodded resignedly. Then he walked over to the old tramp. He stopped momentarily and frowned.

'Is that you Mr Fogg?' he asked.

The tramp glanced up and smiled, 'Mr Froome, of all the people. I thought you were with Lord Boreham.'

'He passed away,' replied Froome, setting the glass and bottle down on a table beside the armchair.

The Englishman poured a generous amount into the glass and took a swig. He savoured the moment and then grinned beatifically.

'That is rather good. Brings back happy more convivial times. Tell me, what on earth possessed your country to take leave of its senses and ban this nectar from the lips of discerning men and women?'

It was a good question and frankly the answer was beyond Flynn. Bobbie decided it was time to build on the rapport she had established with the old tramp.

'Tell me Mr Fogg, what did you see?' asked Bobbie.

This occasioned another mouthful of conviviality. He raised his glass and said, 'I'll wet my whistle.'

'When you're ready,' said Flynn, with more than a trace of irritation, which immediately earned a frown from Bobbie. Behind Flynn, Belmont and the Monk brothers entered the room.

Then, after a few moments reflection, Fogg began.

'I saw the young girls playing together. I remember there was a snowball fight. One of them is a rather good shot, I must say. Saved the other one from a rather vile tempered mutt. They're obviously good friends because they were both laughing. While I was watching, I was aware that there were two men sitting on a park bench nearby. They did not appear to pay much attention to the girls as far as I could see. Then one of them, the smaller of the two, rose and left the park at the exit on 5th Avenue near East 69th.'

'Can you describe them?' interjected Bobbie. 'One was small. The other big?'

'Yes, very big. Well over six feet and large. The other man was perhaps my size, five eight. He was wearing a hat, but I think he removed it briefly and he had pale skin and reddish hair. I would say he was of Irish extraction. I couldn't see what he wore underneath his grey overcoat.'

'And the other man?' asked Flynn, keen to take control of the interview back off his daughter.

'He wore a dark overcoat and looked Russian to me.'

'Russian?' exclaimed Flynn.

'Yes.'

'How?' asked Bobbie, surprised at such a specific response.

'His features were quite Slavic. You know, very prominent cheekbones and slightly angled eyes. Definitely not oriental before you ask. My old master used to deal with many émigrés from Russia after the Revolution. A hard people.'

'So, what happened?' pressed Flynn.

'One of the young girls went off to hide behind a tree while the other appeared to shut her eyes and begin counting. The young girl went off and hid near where the two men had been sitting. I wasn't really paying attention anymore. I do remember seeing the young girl looking for her friend. By then the man who had remained was no longer there. At that point I moved away to the bushes as I had to answer the call of nature. After that I went for a walk. When I came back twenty minutes later there were all these men and policemen shouting out a girl's name.

'Do you think if we took you down to the station you could give a description to a police artist?' asked Flynn.

'May I keep the bottle?' asked Fogg.

'Of course,' said Monk immediately.

'Thank you. In that case I would be happy to help. So, you believe that these beasts have kidnapped the young girl?'

Flynn looked grimly back at the old Englishman and replied, 'It sure looks that way.' Then he turned to the patrolman and added, 'Can you take Mr Fogg to the precinct and show him some photographs. Get a police artist too.'

13

Bobbie followed the policeman and Fogg out of the room before her father could say anything to her. In fact, at that moment, her father was in a quandary. This was the life of a father, to a headstrong daughter of course, being angry and proud in equal measure. He doubted his lot would get any easier, until he did what most men were forced to do in the end. However, he wasn't quite ready to roll the white flag out yet.

'Mr Fogg,' said Bobbie, as he reached the door.

The former butler turned around. Bobbie handed him a piece of paper. Fogg looked at it and he saw on it an address.

'Goodbye Mr Fogg,' said Bobbie.

The old man nodded gratefully and then, with an airy wave of his hand, 'I must fly. We have kidnappers to catch,' he said.

'We do,' said Bobbie as the door closed. As soon as they were gone, Bobbie made a beeline for the kitchen. She wasn't sure what mood her father would be in, so it seemed the safest course of action was to vacate the scene.

Everyone stood up as she entered the kitchen. Bobbie saw the plates on the table and realised they were probably having a quick lunch before they were called back to duty.

'Sit down, don't mind me,' said Bobbie, taking a seat herself. She fixed her attention on Froom. 'Tell me about Mr Fogg. You have obviously met before.'

Froome raised his eyebrows and nodded. He took off his half-moon spectacles and polished them with a napkin.

'It feels like a lifetime ago but yes, we knew one another, professionally, I might add, not personally. We met in England from time to time as my master, Lord Boreham, was involved with the Foreign Office. His master was Lord Leech of Chalfont. We worked together at a number of conferences in London when both gentlemen were attending. I heard that his son died in that terrible war and that he lost his wife, Olive, to Spanish flu. I had no idea that he was in America, though, and in such reduced circumstances.'

'How terrible for him. Do you know if he had any other family?'

'I don't believe so, although in service, one's family tends to be those you work with and for,' explained Froome.

'Who is left in the house from the Monk family?'

'Mrs Monk and Mrs Belmont left earlier. I believe they have gone to Mrs Belmont's apartment. Not surprisingly, Mrs Belmont is in shock. Mr Belmont, young Mr Monk and their two cousins are still with us. Mr St Clair is with Mr Monk'

'Mr St Clair?' asked Bobbie.

'He is the acting chairman of the bank. An old family friend,' responded the butler.

'And their cousins?' asked Bobbie.

Froome's face fell slightly, but he was too professional to allow any personal view to affect his demeanour.

'Yes, Mr Lawrence and Miss Elsbeth Beauregard. They are in the garden now, taking some air.'

Without knowing why, Bobbie rose from the table. The idea of sitting around or, perhaps, being asked to leave by her father, was the last thing she wanted.

'I shall see if they will chat to me, about the late Mr Monk.'

Before Froome, or the kitchen staff, could catch their breath, Bobbie flew out the kitchen door and into the garden. She saw the siblings at the summer house, sitting on the porch. They were wrapped up in overcoats which reminded Bobbie of how cold she was.

Perhaps returning to the scene of the crime, thought Bobbie, before stopping herself. She was not some fictional female sleuth, jumping ahead to solutions, before any evidence had been assembled. The two Beauregards were well wrapped up in overcoats. Bobbie walked up the icy path to the brother and sister and introduced herself.

'Hello, I'm sorry but I don't believe we have met. My name is Roberta Flynn, from the *New York American*. Mr Monk asked me to write a piece on his late father. That's all been turned on its head rather, with this awful business.'

Neither of the Beauregards said anything to this. They continued to eye Bobbie warily, like two vultures, waiting for their prey to expire. Painfully.

Bobbie controlled her annoyance and pressed on regardless. If they were going to be rude, then it would excuse the white lie that she was about to tell. Of course, no woman ever tells a lie. It is understood that truth is not just about proof or perception, it is also about perspective. From a woman's perspective, she is telling the truth and *that,* is all there is to it.

'Mr Monk asked me to speak to you about his late father,' said Bobbie. This had the virtue of not being an outright falsehood, although it probably was stretching the truth, somewhat.

'I'm surprised,' said the young woman who would have been rather attractive had it not been for the sneer. She was around Bobbie's age and spoke with a southern accent.

'Why do you say that Miss...?' prompted Bobbie.

'Beauregard,' answered Elspeth. 'I'm not sure it's really your business or, for that matter, your readers.'

'I see,' said Bobbie. 'Do you have any memories of your uncle that could be shared?'

'No,' answered Elspeth firmly.

Bobbie felt like she was accelerating quickly towards a dead end. She thought quickly and then said, 'I gather this is where he passed away.' She indicated with her eyes the room behind the siblings.

'Shot himself, you mean,' replied Lawrence. He, too, had a sneer rippling through his southern accent.

'I gather that's what the inquest said,' replied Bobbie, placing as much scepticism as she could into her voice. It was time to stretch the truth a little further. She fixed her eyes on the brother and said, 'You realise, of course, that the kidnapping will perhaps bring about a review of what happened that awful day.'

This had the desired effect. The two Beauregards sat upright, as if someone had given them a mild electric shock.

'What do you mean?'

Bobbie was ready for this. Her eyes narrowed as she went in for the kill.

'Well, I gather that anyone who was here that day might be asked a few questions, original statements reviewed. I think there was not much by way of an investigation originally. There will be now.'

This news seemed to be about as welcome as dandruff to the siblings. They shifted in their seats uncomfortably, before Lawrence tried to get back on the front foot.

'What's all this to you?'

Bobbie dealt with this easily, 'Like you, I just want to see the safe return of the child. That is the priority. I imagine the police will view it that way too. I'm sure the kidnapping and the suicide are not connected, but every avenue will need to be explored. Can I ask where you were when Mr Monk passed away?'

'The library.'

'None of your business.'

The two Beauregards spoke at the same time before glaring at one another. Elspeth, who had mentioned the library, continued.

'We were in the library,' she said, ignoring her brother's angry look.

Bobbie decided to take a risk. Faint heart never won fair story, thought Bobbie.

'And the arguments?'

Bobbie had no idea if there had been any arguments that day, but in a family such as this, with very powerful personalities, it was a reasonable bet that there were.

'How did you...?' began Elspeth before being silenced by her brother touching her hand.

Bobbie looked at them expectantly, but Elspeth did not add anything to this. Still, it was something. The gamble had paid off and Bobbie knew what she would do next.

She smiled to the Beauregards and said, 'I won't take up any more of your time. Thank you for your help.' She tried not to make that last comment too arch but knew she had failed dismally when she saw the flash of anger in Lawrence's eyes. He was a rather insecure young man, which was a pity, because he was unquestionably, like the two Monk brothers, rather good-looking. Bobbie could imagine many southern belles who might fall for him. Good luck to them. He had a rather unfortunate combination of arrogance and weakness, which Bobbie detested in men when it was not, at least, leavened by either some form of self-awareness or a sense of humour.

The odd pair had given her food for thought though. There had clearly been tension in the air at the house. Perhaps this was not unusual, but she could not assume this. She desperately needed to understand why there had been conflict on that particular day. The people most likely to know were the principals, of course. Bobbie marched back up the garden towards the house. There was another potential source for this information and she was just outside the room where she would find them.

14

It was a sign of just how miserable Violet felt that the appearance of Renat represented something to be glad about. This did not quite make her Pollyanna, but it did make her feel a little less abandoned and she'd had quite enough of that to last a lifetime. Still, it was not in her character to make anything easy for anyone, especially kidnappers.

'What do you want,' she snapped at him.

The force of her hatred almost jolted Renat. If he'd had doubts about this plan beforehand, then he was feeling it doubly now. Something in the girl's insistence that they had the wrong person, was beginning to worry him. Unlike Bugsy, he was inclined to believe her. Where he had come from, trust was a rare commodity and truth barely existed. Yet when you saw it, or heard it spoken, then you instinctively understood when you were in its presence.

The young girl's attitude towards them had changed subtly over the few hours they had been together. Initially, she had been angry. This was no surprise. No child likes to have their play interrupted, whether it is by parents or, in this case, evil kidnappers. Then as realisation dawned on her, she had clearly felt fear at what might become of her. Now Renat could see that her manner had shifted once more to another emotion.

Contempt.

Not just common-or-garden contempt of I-don't-like-you. Nothing so simple. This hell-child was actually displaying every sign that she thought the two men ludicrous. The reason for this was not hard to fathom if one viewed it through the lens that he, Renat, had simply snatched the wrong girl.

And Renat was not completely convinced that he had taken the right girl. It was an easy mistake to make. They looked quite similar and no one had had the sense to give him a photograph of their target. In fact, anticipating the anger that Bugsy was bound to feel, he would point out to his partner-in-crime that he was equally culpable. Bugsy should have pointed to the girl he wanted. In truth, he suspected that Bugsy had no more idea than he and had simply avoided taking responsibility.

He threw a pastrami sandwich onto the bed.

'Eat,' he ordered, more in hope than expectation. He suspected that the imp would simply hurl it back in his face.

She looked down at the roll. She was hungry. Very hungry. Equally, she did not want to seem indebted for the food. What to do?

'What is it?'

'Pastrami,' said the loquacious Russian.

She quite liked pastrami. There seemed nothing else to do. She picked up the sandwich and said absently, 'Thanks.'

'Okay,' responded the Russian, before realising that the conversation was bordering on the absurd. He left the room to join his partner who was pacing up and down, smoking his tenth cigarette in as many minutes. Bugsy was not a patient man. Renat had the patience borne of years of long, cold and dark nights in his homeland. The Russian winter bred nothing else.

Half an hour later, Bugsy appeared in the room. He was wearing an overcoat and he had a small coat draped over his arm which Violet took to be for her. She was rather glad to see this as the room was cold and she had been shivering quite violently. The last thing she'd wanted to do was ask her captors for anything.

Bugsy handed her the coat and said, 'Put it on.'

'I'm hardly going to set fire to it,' snapped Violet back. It was one of the less attractive aspects of her precocity, that she had a fairly robust and highly developed sense of sarcasm.

Bugsy snarled at her and raised his hand, before stopping himself. His father had spent most of his early life hitting him, whenever the mood took him. While Bugsy was no stranger to violence, he'd sworn to himself that he would not do this with kids as his father had done.

Bugsy glared down at her. 'Get up,' he ordered, but felt it necessary to grab her arm anyway, anticipating some pointless act of rebellion.

Violet was too cold, tired and bored to argue the point. She spun off the bed and stood up, rather unsteadily, making sure to return Bugsy's stare.

Bugsy led her into the sparsely furnished living room. There was a candlestick telephone sitting on a table. Bugsy went over to it and picked up the phone. Renat, sitting on a wooden chair, yawned.

Violet listened as Bugsy asked to be put through to the Monk household. As he waited for a connection to be made, he shielded the mouthpiece with his hand and said to the young girl, 'When I say speak, you speak, understand?'

Violet nodded. Then a thought occurred to her and she asked, 'What do I say?'

Bugsy evidently hadn't given any thought to this and he glanced in the direction of the big Russian for inspiration. Unfortunately, just at that moment Renat was picking food out of his teeth so Bugsy abandoned that avenue of stimulus and thought for a moment.

'Tell them you are alive.'

'I think they'll work that out for themselves, when I speak,' pointed out Violet.

Bugsy was sorely tempted to lash out, but he gritted his teeth and said, 'Fine, say that you miss them and they are to do as the man says.'

The chance to deploy her venomous humour gave her a lift. She felt her spirits rise. She put a hand on her hip and said, 'If I don't?'

'I'll hit you and that'll probably make you scream. Your folks will recognise your scream, believe me and they'll pay double what we want. Your choice, kid. Choose wisely.'

Violet held the kidnapper's gaze and nodded slowly.

'Why are you calling Mr Monk, though? He's not my dad.'

'Don't be funny kid....hello?' said Bugsy as a voice came on the line.

'Listen hard, I'm only going to say this once. We have your daughter,' said Bugsy, in what he hoped was a voice full of threat. This was undermined a moment later.

'You don't,' pointed out Jefferson Monk at the other end of the line. 'You have my lawyer's daughter Violet. I demand you return her immediately.'

'Don't lie,' shouted Bugsy. 'We have your daughter and if you want to see her again alive then you'll do as I say. We want two hundred thousand dollars in used notes and we want it tomorrow.'

'What?' exclaimed Monk at the other end of the line.

'You heard.'

'How do we know Violet is even alive?'

Bugsy thrust the phone in the direction of Violet and pointed to her threateningly.

'Hello, Mr Monk,' said Violet with an unnaturally calm voice that gave Bugsy some reassurance that his threat had worked. He would be swiftly disabused of this hope in a few moments as Violet had deliberately led him into a false sense of security.

'These bozos have the wrong girl,' said the little she-devil.

Oddly, both Jefferson Monk and Renat, the Russian, could not have agreed more on this and for reasons beyond the obvious point that she was not the banker's daughter.

'We'll get you back honey...' replied Monk. The phone was ripped from Violet's fingers and a stinging slap sent her flying to the ground. She let out a scream which led Monk to shout, 'Hey, what's going on there?'

'Get the money, creep, or your daughter gets it,' snarled Bugsy.

'She's not...' but Monk was cut off in his prime by Bugsy replacing the receiver.

Bugsy stalked forward and stood over the crying child who was cowering in the corner.

'You do that once more kid and, I promise you, you won't see your folks again.'

With that he grabbed Violet by the arm and virtually hurled her back into the room. Then he turned around and saw Renat, shaking his head slowly at him. He waved the big

Russian away and said, 'To hell with you too. I'm going out. I need some fresh air. Punk kid better watch out.'

Renat watched him go and then stood up. He walked over to the room where Violet was sobbing on the other side of the door.

He knocked on the door.

Violet's two word reply coincidentally were the first two words that Renat had learned in English. Oddly, he was quite impressed with the little girl's spirit, as well as her command of the darker regions of her native language.

15

Bobbie entered through the kitchen door and found Eileen, the cook, being helped by Mary, to make sandwiches for the various family members and their guests from the NYPD. There was an intoxicating aroma of fresh bread, baking in the oven. It reminded her of Mrs Garcia's bread, their housekeeper and cook. She had to learn how to make bread from this lady. Her mother had never been much of a dab hand in the kitchen. Her father didn't mind, though. She had been a beauty. Bobbie found it difficult to breathe for a moment, as she remembered her mother. How she missed her.

It was just a momentary pause. It was too cold to stop anywhere long, especially without a coat. She continued into the kitchen. The two ladies stopped what they were doing when Bobbie arrived. Bobbie waved at them to continue.

'Don't mind me. My that bread sure smells good.'

'You should try some,' said Eileen with a proud grin. This was exactly what Bobbie had been angling for. She had a charming lack of scruples when it came to getting her way. Eileen handed her some warm buttered bread which Bobbie gratefully accepted.

'May I ask you a couple of questions while you work?' asked Bobbie, in a manner of someone who has suddenly just had a thought occur to them. It always worked and did so here.

'Of course,' said Eileen. The cook was built exactly as one would want. Her girth was barely contained behind her pinny.

'Did you see Mr Monk on that fateful day?' asked Bobbie.

'We did,' replied Eileen speaking for herself and Mary.

'Did you speak with him?'

'Oh yes, he sometimes came into the kitchen to do just what you're doing miss, often with Mr St Clair,' grinned Eileen. Her smile was wistful and Bobbie realised she had to tread carefully.

'You miss him, don't you?'

The two ladies stopped making the sandwiches and nodded.

'He was always lovely with us,' said Mary, speaking for the first time. She had an Irish accent, which surprised Bobbie.

'He was. He may have been tough with a few of the family, but with us he was never less than appreciative,' agreed Eileen.

'Tough with the family?' asked Bobbie, trying to appear guileless. 'Were there many arguments on that day?'

'Well, it seemed to me young Mr Monk and his father were always arguing and they certainly had a bit of a barney that day. I don't know why. He was in a bit of a bad mood anyway because his wife's niece and nephew were visiting.'

'There wasn't much love there?' asked Bobbie, stealing another bit of bread which made the two ladies smile.

'No. Not much. I don't think Mrs Monk has much time for them either. Always after some money as far as I can tell.'

'Why were they here? Do they visit frequently?'

'Usually when they need money.'

'I would have thought, as a family lawyer, Mr Belmont would be a frequent visitor,' said Bobbie.

'He is, well his wife is. The two children love playing together,' said Mary. She stopped for a moment as her emotions got the better of her. Bobbie put her hand over the young woman's hand and said, 'Don't worry. They're doing everything they can to find her. My dad won't sleep until she's back with Mrs Belmont.'

The two ladies nodded at this and seemed more hopeful. Bobbie gazed out the window at the two siblings who were sitting in silence.

'Why would the Beauregards have come all the way up here on that day, just because a lawyer was visiting his client?'

'Perhaps they had heard that Mr Belmont was here to discuss the will.'

Bobbie thought this unlikely, for a number of reasons. Firstly, and most obviously, how would they have heard, unless one of their cousins had told them. Or, perhaps, Belmont himself? The second thought was one she could, at least, check on with the two ladies.

'I thought the Beauregard family were well off, why would they be anxious about any change in the will?' prompted Bobbie.

'They were, I suppose. Old money. Not much of it left I gather and Mr Monk was always having to pay for them. He did it for his wife but, since she became ill...'

Eileen paused at this point and tears formed in her eyes. She shrugged and Bobbie decided there was nothing to be gained by pressing the point much further.

'This bread is rather gorgeous,' replied Bobbie stealing one last bit of it which brought a chuckle from the two ladies. 'If you'll excuse me, I'll head back to the others. I hope they've made some progress.'

Just as she was about to leave, a tall, well-dressed man entered the kitchen and greeted the ladies.

'Good afternoon, Mr St Clair,' responded Eileen.

'Hello Eileen,' said St Clair. He had a melancholic smile on his face. 'I thought I'd pop down for old times' sake. The smell of your bread bewitched me, as ever.'

Bobbie put St Clair as being in his late sixties. He had a kindly, albeit patrician, air. This man was old money in a young country. He paused and looked at Bobbie for a moment because that was what all men, and most women, did when they saw the combination of beauty and auburn hair.

Eileen stepped into the fray to explain Bobbie's presence.

'Miss Flynn is a journalist here to write a story on Mr Monk. She has similar tastes to yourself and Mr...' she paused at this moment as she remembered her late master. Bobbie stood up immediately and took her hand. It was an instinctive gesture and one that immediately impressed St Clair.

'We all miss him,' said St Clair. 'None more so than you, Eileen, I'm sure.'

Eileen nodded, unable to speak. Then she smiled through the tears that had formed in her eyes.

'Well, I think I know what you are here for Mr St Clair.'

St Clair laughed. It was a pleasant sound and Bobbie decided she liked the man. He nodded, 'May I?'

Mary cut him a piece of bread and lashed an unhealthy amount of butter on it. St Clair's eyes lit up as he saw the butter immediately begin to melt into the warm bread.

'It's delicious,' confirmed Bobbie.

St Clair was too much of a gentleman to say, "so are you" but, alas, men are weak and such a thought did cross his mind, briefly. He smiled back and asked Bobbie about how her piece was progressing.

'It was going well up until the horrible news about Violet Belmont. How are Mr and Mrs Belmont? I can't imagine how they must be feeling'.

'Nor I,' agreed St Clair before trying the bread. He almost groaned with pleasure but did shut his eyes and became six years old again. When he had finished, 'Yes, awful business. This house has almost become cursed.' Bobbie could not believe that such a man was superstitious and St Clair quickly added, 'Of course, that is nonsense, but so much tragedy in such a short space of time.'

'How long had you known Mr Monk?' asked Bobbie.

'Ten years, perhaps longer. It was through work initially, but we seemed to share a similar outlook on life and we became good friends. I miss him.'

'It must have been a shock for you, too,' said Bobbie, gently.

'Yes and no. His life changed as Mrs Monk's illness became more acute. It was heart breaking to see. Perhaps it was not such a surprise as we think.'

Bobbie decided that to push any further, in the circumstances, would be insensitive. She rose from her seat and shook hands with St Clair.

'It was nice to meet you Mr St Clair, I'm just sorry it was under such dreadful circumstances. My condolences for your loss.'

She said her goodbyes to the staff and left the kitchen. The first person that she ran into as she headed up the corridor was Detective Nolan.

'There you are,' said Nolan, in a manner that Bobbie suspected did not augur well for her continued presence in the house.

'Before you throw me out into the street, Detective Nolan, I've been asking some questions about the death of Mr Monk.'

This was greeted, not surprisingly, by a frown from the young detective. Just as he was about to respond, Bobbie cut him off and continued. He seemed to accept this gracefully enough, which led Bobbie to assume he had a woman in his life. He was clearly quite well trained when it came to staying quiet while a woman spoke. It made Bobbie wonder if he was married or had a sweetheart.

'Apparently there were arguments that morning between Monk the elder and the youngest son. Given that we know Mr Belmont was at the house that day to discuss the will, I think...'

'...it proves nothing,' finished Nolan.

Bobbie's face fell at this. It was difficult to argue this point, so she did not try. Further up the corridor, she saw the two Monk brothers with Fitzroy Belmont. They were leaving the study and walking into the dining room. Her father was with them.

'Did he send you to find me?' asked Bobbie, glancing up at Nolan.

Nolan half-smiled before saying, 'You should be a detective.' Bobbie was not entirely sure if this was serious, a joke or a bit of both. Froome appeared in the corridor and walked towards them.

'Are you joining the gentlemen for lunch?' asked Froome.

'No, I shall be on my way soon,' said Bobbie and was a little gratified to see a look of sadness of the face of the kindly butler.

'We shall be sorry to see you go,' said Froome. He continued on his way to the kitchen, leaving Bobbie and Nolan alone in the corridor.

'Well, I think you have your man now,' observed Bobbie to Nolan. 'I'll come quietly. No need for handcuffs.'

This final comment was said with a wicked enough grin to make the detective wonder exactly what was being said, but he decided not to respond in kind. Instead, he glanced with his eyes towards the door.

Bobbie shrugged and the two headed up the corridor passing the study on their way. The door to the study was open. Lying on the office table were some documents. Bobbie stopped for a moment as she gazed into the room. Then she turned to Nolan, mischief in her eyes.

'You don't suppose that's the will, do you?'

16

With Bugsy away, the mood in the house appeared to lighten. Renat was never going to be best friend material for Violet, but he was a good sight better company than the permanently peeved Bugsy. Renat did not lock the young girl in her room, so she went into the living room, sat down on a cushion on the floor and read the previous day's *New York Times*. She loved to read the paper. Renat looked down at her reading the paper and asked her the question uppermost in his mind.

'So, you're not the daughter?'

'No,' replied Violet eyeing the Russian closely. 'Why doesn't your friend believe me?'

Renat shrugged. Man's capacity for delusion knew no bounds. This was one insight he'd gained from his thirty-six years on the planet. While he had no illusions about how hard life was, he was rarely surprised when he saw how gullible men could be: they followed dreams that were folly, leaders who were fools and gods who had abandoned them. One cold winter in Arctic Circle Russia would swiftly correct any misapprehension that life was anything but pain and suffering, with occasional moments of luck. Fatalism was Renat's religion and he was a faithful adherent to its cold, callous, conscience-free reality.

In this, he would have found accord from a surprising source. The young girl who fate, and a two hundred dollars down-payment, had thrown his way was no stranger to the slings and arrows that life could hurl malevolently in your direction. If he had known then, it certainly would have explained her rather phlegmatic reaction to a rather uncommon situation.

'They won't pay, you know,' said Violet, not looking up from the paper. 'I mean, why should they?' She looked wistful for a moment. Perhaps this was the only time she had seemed to dwell on any self-pity. Quietly, without any rancour she said, 'It's not as if I'm their daughter.'

If what she said was true, and Renat, by now, certainly believed every word she said, it was difficult to argue that she was right.

'Maybe your father pay instead?' suggested Renat.

Just for a moment, Renat could swear she saw tears form in her eyes, but she looked away and said, 'He doesn't have that much money.'

'Someone pay?' asked Renat, hopefully. In truth, he was something of a novice in the area of abduction. His forte tended more towards violence or, more usually, its threat. He had lost count of the men he had killed in the war and it had been at least a year since he had last seen any of their faces in his dreams. He had become completely immune to guilt and had never given much thought to the morality of his chosen profession.

'No one pay,' said Violet, adopting the argot of her captor. 'No. One.'

This sounded less than hopeful. Renat's heart sank a little. He would be blamed for the mistake. Months, perhaps years of planning for all he knew, had been wiped out by a simple lapse. He did not blame himself. Why should he? Failure was as inevitable a part of his life as punishment. Both would come his way.

He would be ready.

Violet looked up at him and felt some sympathy which surprised her. Renat looked utterly miserable.

'Will you be blamed for this, Renat? It is Renat, isn't it?'

Renat nodded.

'Well look, Renat. I've been thinking. If you're going to get the blame for lifting the wrong girl, then why not go the whole hog and let me go?'

This made Renat smile. She had spirit, he gave her that. He could see it in her eyes, on the firm set of the mouth and the straight back. She was a fighter. This was unusual for someone born into such a wealthy background.

'*Niet.*'

Well even if she did not speak Russian, this sounded like a 'no' in any language and a hard, Russian 'no' did not brook argument, even from a precocious ten-year-old.

'Where's your friend?' asked Violet. 'He's gonna be disappointed if he thinks there's no money coming his way.'

Renat was not going to dispute that, so resorted once more to a shrug.

'You have any kids Renat?' asked Violet. She was genuinely curious.

The big Russian looked away from the little girl. His eyes gazed at the wall, but what they saw was not the paint peeling from the walls. They saw beyond the wall to a land far off and a time when his life had been very different. He saw a woman standing in a field. An icy wind pinching her face. Her hands were caressing her stomach.

So long ago.

He awoke from the reverie when he felt a hand on his. The child's hand. He realised there were tears in his eyes because he couldn't see her clearly. He wiped his eyes and glared at the young girl. She glared back at him.

'Why are you so sad?' she asked.

He shook his head and pointed to the bedroom.

'Rest,' he said.

Under any normal circumstances, she would have stayed and argued the point. How parents loved that. Something made her get to her feet, though. She felt she had intruded on something she did not understand and it made her feel sad too.

Inside the room, she went over to the bed. Rather than lie down, she stood at the window and looked out. A light snow was falling. The view from the window was a tiny back yard with a high wall. Violet looked at the wall. It was too high to climb. But then how would she even get outside?

Without knowing why, she put her hands on the windowsill and tried to lift the window. It wouldn't budge. She tried a little bit harder.

It shifted.

Slightly.

Confused, Violet put all her strength into lifting it a bit more. It rose another few inches. Cold air invaded the room. Rather than push the window up higher, she pulled it down again. Then she went over to the bed and lay down.

Violet Belmont was, she knew, a difficult child. For as long as she could remember, she'd had few friends. She was different. Smarter. Much smarter than others. The only one who had ever accepted her, accepted *this*, was Lydia Monk. She thought of her friend now and tears formed in her eye. It was not for herself though. It was almost relief that it was she who had been taken and not her friend. She was glad that, in some way, she had saved her friend from this ordeal. She loved her friend, but she would not have coped. Not Lydia. Violet knew she wasn't just smarter. She was stronger too. Stronger because she had not been born into wealth. Far from it.

The thought boosted her spirit at that moment and fuelled something else. A plan was forming in Violet's mind. Violet Belmont was a difficult child.

Different.
Stronger.
Smarter.

17

'Don't even think about it,' said Nolan in an urgent whisper. Bobbie pretended not to hear him. Her eyes were fixed on the documents sitting on the table. She turned to him. There was a set look in her green eyes. Nolan knew his petition was doomed to failure; from the moment the thought had formed in her head. He could see it on her face and he rather liked what he saw, too. But this was madness.

Bobbie darted into the room before Nolan could stop her, although he doubted he would have tried to restrain her. She was over by the table staring down at the file.

THE LAST WILL AND TESTAMENT OF HAMILTON LEWIS MONK

'Don't,' repeated Nolan in a whisper, but this was distinctly less insistent.

'Keep an eye on the door,' ordered Bobbie and, much to her surprise and Nolan's shock, he complied. This young girl was impossible he decided. Utterly, irretrievably impossible.

'What does it say?' said Nolan, one eye peeking out from behind the door into the corridor. His scruples had fallen faster than a floozy's drawers at an orgy.

Bobbie eyes quickly scanned past the legalese to the business end of the will. She said, 'There are quite a few beneficiaries. Some charities. Those awful cousins didn't get much. Ten thousand dollars each.'

'Sounds plenty to me,' said Nolan, grimly.

'Most of the money goes to the two sons and the houses to his wife. The staff get some money too. Froome has a house for life and a couple of thousand with it. Very nice for him.'

There were noises in the corridor.

'Hurry,' urged Nolan.

It was Froome and Mary bringing trays of sandwiches for the men in the dining room. Augustus St Clair was with them. He was even carrying a tray. They entered the dining room.

'Interesting,' said Bobbie staring down at the will, then she closed it over.

'What was?' asked Nolan turning to her.

Before Bobbie could answer, there was some noise from the dining room. Bobbie quickly scurried over to Nolan. They nipped out into the corridor just as the door of the dining room opened.

A man stepped out.

It was her father. He had found her once more. Flynn's piercing eyes glared at Bobbie and Nolan. If pushed, Bobbie would have described his countenance as particularly stony at that moment and his tone had a certain finality to it.

'Bobbie, you have to go. I can't have you wandering around here in the middle of this crisis,' he said, in a low voice full of intent.

He stood for a second and then, reluctantly, Bobbie turned in the direction of the door. She opened it then turned to her father.

'I'm right, you know. I think the kidnapping and the suicide, or murder, are connected.'

With that she walked out the door. In another room, one that she had not been in, she heard Jefferson Monk shout although the tone was tinged with regret, 'You know why I can't pay!'

The door closed behind her. The sight in front of the house almost made her jaw drop.

Inside the house, Flynn felt deflated. He never liked to argue with Bobbie and he both sensed, and understood, her frustration. The fact was, she had been a help to them with the old butler. Her questioning had been astute and sympathetic. This raised two thoughts in his head. He'd never given much credence to the idea of women joining the police, but was he wrong-headed to be opposed? It seemed as if the police were missing out on a resource that they badly needed. More worryingly, he had to acknowledge that Bobbie was more than a chip off the old block. She'd extracted more from Fogg in minutes than he would have obtained in an hour. Flynn glanced up at Nolan and scowled. The young detective was looking at him with a half-smile.

'Wipe that smile off your face, unless you want to be on the street again, son.'

With that Flynn stalked off, past the room where the heated discussion between Monk and someone on the telephone was taking place. Nolan stepped forward towards the door of the office to listen in.

'I'm sorry, Teddy,' said Monk. 'I'm not paying it. That's final. You know why.'

It was in a state of shock at overhearing this that Bobbie found herself on the front steps. Then she had her second shock. She saw immediately why her father had insisted she leave. Standing at the end of the path were around a dozen newsmen. She recognised almost all of them. This made her smile. She turned to the window of the drawing room and saw her father there. He nodded to her then turned away.

It hit Bobbie immediately. The reason why the newsmen were there was because they had been alerted by the door-to-door search, and questioning, for the kidnapped girl. Bobbie felt herself standing up to her full five feet three and then she marched down the short path. Her appearance was greeted with a mixture of groans and shouts.

'Come on Red, give us a break. What's happening?' shouted one. Then the others joined in.

Another shouted, 'Who's taken the Monk kid?'

'Sorry boys,' said Bobbie grinning, 'You can read all about it in this evening's paper.' Then, she stopped and looked at the newsman who had asked about the Monk kid. Her head was spinning now.

They thought it was Lydia Monk who had been kidnapped.

She hurried past the waiting reporters and went straight over to a yellow taxicab, which had just dropped off another reporter.

'Hey Red,' shouted the newsman exiting the cab, 'Where are you goin'?'

'To post a scoop, Brad,' said Bobbie to the newsman, before climbing into the cab and out of the noise and the chilly air. She leaned forward to the driver and said, 'Get to the Tribune building on Park Road, quick. There's a tip in it for you.'

The cab driver was a man named Jimmy Kinsella. He was a man that loved many things in life, specifically, broads, booze and big bills, in that order. He also loved to drive fast. Getting paid to do exactly what he loved doing anyway, was just one of the many perks of his job.

'Hold onto your hat lady,' he said and slammed his foot down on the accelerator, sending Bobbie flying forward and then back.

'Thattaboy,' shouted Bobbie gleefully.

It's hard to say how many traffic violations Jimmy committed in his record-breaking sprint to Park Road, but he would be in his favourite speakeasy that night boasting of the near misses and the big tip, he received from an absolute doll of a reporter.

Bobbie hopped out of the cab as Jimmy pulled up to a halt outside the Tribune building, with enough of a screech to attract the attention of one policeman and four nearby poodles, who immediately began yelping in anger.

'Thanks Jimmy,' shouted Bobbie.

'Anytime, Red,' shouted Jimmy, who then tore off, lest the policeman take any further interest in his speeding.

Bobbie ran into the building and skipped up the stairs to the second floor. She entered the newsroom like a mini hurricane and made straight for Thornton Kent's office. He was in a meeting with his secretary. Bobbie knocked once and then pushed the door open.

'Guess where I've just come from?'

Kent was too angry to reply. His eyes widened and Bobbie could have sworn she saw his nostrils flare. Rather than risk being hurled out of the window by an angry editor, Bobbie felt the best course of action would be to answer her own question.

'I've just come back from the Monk house. I was interviewing Jefferson Monk when the kidnapping occurred. I have the scoop.'

Kent sat up and, immediately, his face became hungry. A predator. For news.

'Go on, what's the scoop? Every man and his dog knows the Monk kid has been kidnapped.'

Bobbie leaned forward and looked Kent right in the eye.

'She hasn't.'

Kent was confused by this and then wondered if Bobbie had taken leave of her senses.

'It's not Lydia Monk. It's her friend Violet Belmont. They took the wrong girl, and they're demanding two hundred thousand dollars as a ransom. Two men. One small, the other big and he might be Russian. There was a witness.'

'Get this down.'

'Front page?' pushed Bobbie.

'Get out of here,' shouted Kent at the departing Bobbie, who had wisely turned tail as soon as she demanded the front page. He heard her laughing as she ran out of the office.

Bobbie took Kent's reaction as a 'yes'. Rather than go to the Obits office, she found a spare desk and immediately began to type up a report on what had happened. Unfortunately, Damon Runyon was not around to help add some polish to what she had written, but she knew just where to find him. It was now a little after two in the afternoon. It took Bobbie thirty minutes to complete the report to her satisfaction. She saw Kent standing at the window of his office with brow furrowed, so deep it might have struck oil.

With something of a flourish, Bobbie pulled the paper from the typewriter and marched into Kent's office. He snatched the report from her, before he could start to read it, he was distracted by the sound of the office door closing. This was another moment when he questioned the sanity of the young woman. Usually, she would stand over him arguing over every syllable.

He ran to the door and shouted, 'Where are you off to?'

'Print what you want,' shouted Bobbie airily. 'I have a lead to follow up.'

18

Outside the Tribune building, Bobbie hailed a cab and asked to go to 1626 Broadway at NE corner of 49th Street. They drove up 8th Avenue and the cabbie did not stop for breath while complaining about the amount of traffic. Bobbie was more concerned how much money she had, as the cost of the ride escalated. After a twenty-minute ride, she was able to decamp from the car when they reached her destination.

Lindy's.

Lindy's was a restaurant that had opened the previous year. The owner was Leo "Lindy" Lindemann who, along with his wife Clara, had created a home from home for the Broadway crowd. This was an ill-assorted group of men and women who included in their number, reporters, card players, horseplayers, bookies, song-pluggers, agents, actors in and out of work, as well as members of the Mafia.

Bobbie breezed into the restaurant and caught sight of Runyon sitting with a couple of gentlemen, one of whom was small and dressed very sharply, which is to say he looked like a mobster and the other was large, with a nose that had clearly come out the wrong wide of an argument with a knuckleduster.

Bobbie waved over at Runyon, who was tucking into a dish of ham hock and sauerkraut. Runyon motioned for her to join them. There was no room to stand up, so Bobbie fell into the seat beside Runyon and waited expectantly to be introduced.

'Gentlemen, meet Red. She is an ace reporter at the *New York American*. You'll be hearing a lot of her soon.'

Bobbie glanced archly in Runyon's direction, but to be fair, there had been no trace of irony in his voice. He genuinely meant it.

'We are pleased to meet you, Red,' said the smaller of the two men. 'My name is Arnold and this is my associate, Lenny.'

Arnold made Lenny sound like a business partner, when a more accurate assessment would have been bodyguard. He was built like a heavyweight boxer, with a face that looked as if he used his head rather than his gloves to defend himself.

The Arnold in question was someone Bobbie recognised immediately. He was Arnold Rothstein, the head of the Jewish Mafia. Bobbie was unsure whether to be nervous about this or not but, as he seemed quite at ease, then she decided she could be too. Besides which, it was always difficult to feel threatened by anyone wearing a polka dot bow tie. It was too much like a bow a girl might wear. Rothstein looked to be in his mid-forties. His dark hair was receding a little at the temples which was only emphasised by the fact that he combed it over from the side.

'What brings you here, Red?' asked Runyon, dabbing the side of his mouth.

'I've just come from the Monk house, have you heard what's happened?' asked Bobbie.

'Some wise guys swiped his kid,' replied Runyon. He turned to face her.

'Not quite. They took the wrong kid,' pointed out Bobbie. 'Now they want nearly quarter of a million and they're not going to get it.'

'Any ideas on who would commit such a foul and nasty piece of work?' asked Rothstein.

'There was a witness. He saw two men: one was small with reddish hair underneath his hat and the other was a real big guy who looked Russian,' said Bobbie, stealing a bit of ham from Runyon's plate.

'Renat the Russian,' said the three men in unison.

'Renat the Russian?' repeated Bobbie. She took a notebook out of her pocket and wrote this down.

'Any idea where I can find Mr Renat?' asked Bobbie.

'Any idea where I can find Mr Renat?' repeated Rothstein. He wore a wide grin and glanced towards Runyon. 'Damon, where do you find such a sweet girl as this? Mr Renat. That's good.'

Runyon smiled and then replied, 'Before you go all sweet on Red let me give you her full name, Miss Roberta Flynn. That surname ring a bell with you Arthur?'

'I know there is an officer of the law by that name. Inspector Flynn,' replied Rothstein, still smiling.

'Meet his daughter,' replied Runyon beaming proudly at Bobbie, as if she was his favoured niece.

Rothstein regarded Bobbie for a moment and then said, 'I am telling you; I sure do not see a likeness. You take after your mother.'

Something in Bobbie's face betrayed her sadness at hearing her mother mentioned. Rothstein was immediately contrite.

'My dear, I hope I have not offended you?' said the mobster. He reached out and took Bobbie's hand. It was a nice gesture and utterly at odds with his fearsome reputation.

Bobbie shook her head. She shrugged and sketched a weak smile, 'I lost her a couple of years ago. I miss her.'

'I miss my mother too,' said Rothstein. 'Now, I do not want you to fret. Taking a kid from her family is wrong. I do not like this, see? I will find out where Renat and this other guy is. Have no fear. We will find the kid and we will make a mighty big example of Renat and his friend.'

This sounded ominous but, then again, those who live by the sword...she stopped herself giving this more thought. Hopefully, the men who had abducted Violet would be brought to justice, but the safety of the child was paramount.

'Lenny,' said Rothstein, 'Can you assist this lady and put the word out? Find Renat. Tell them Mr Rothstein is very desirous to meet said Renat. Confirm that said Renat is in very deep...,' Rothstein paused at that moment and recalibrated what he was about to say. 'Trouble.'

19

While Bobbie was spending time with Arnold "the Brain" Rothstein, a man that her father would gladly have put in prison because he was widely suspected of having been the mastermind behind the "Black Sox Scandal", where eight members of the Chicago White Sox were bribed to throw the World Series baseball game, Inspector Flynn was in the middle of a situation that had become, if possible, even more tense.

'What do you mean you won't pay?' asked Flynn, as he faced Jefferson Monk in his office.

'Just that. I think what I've stated is unambiguous,' said Monk, drawing himself up and looking resolute.

'Won't pay or can't pay,' pressed Flynn.

'Both. Even if I had the money I wouldn't pay. It's not my child and frankly it is a ludicrous amount of money. We would be ruined financially because, trust me Inspector, insurance companies don't pay out on kidnap and they certainly don't pay out when you gift your lawyer quarter of a mill to have his daughter released. It's completely absurd and I can tell you, absolutely out of the question.'

'Is Mr Belmont aware of your position on this?' asked Detective Nolan, who had been standing by the door, listening to the exchange.

Monk glared at the young detective who, Flynn noted with some satisfaction, glared right back at him.

'He is, for what it is worth. And, yes, he has made representations to me, but my position is clear and will not change,' replied Monk in a low, intense voice.

The representations Monk spoke of had involved the lawyer begging the head of the bank to change his mind. Monk was unmoved or, at least, would not alter his position. Belmont realised that it was useless to plead any case. In fact, he understood completely the banker's position. How could he forget those damning words?

'Fitzroy, I'm not paying it. That's final. You know why,' he'd shouted. This comment had been heard by Bobbie, her father and Nolan. They had not heard what Monk said next. His words had, effectively, condemned Violet to the mercy of her captors.

'You know why,' Monk had repeated in a lower voice. 'She's not my daughter. Hell, Fitzroy, she's not even yours. You and Olivia adopted her. Or fostered her, whatever you call it. She was abandoned once. The kid's used to it.'

Before Flynn could dispense a few thoughts of his own on the subject, Monk clearly read the intention on the old detective's face.

'I know what you are about to say,' said Monk. 'The kid hasn't a chance if I don't pay. Well for all you know Violet may be dead, and even if she isn't, the plain fact is that they'll realise the game is up. If I tell them I'm not going to pay, then they'll give her up. Why would they want to murder her? I've told Teddy. She's with Olivia now. I've told Fitzroy. He knows my position. I won't change. Why should I? I mean if I pay what's to stop anyone lifting a kid and then demanding some rich guy to ante up? It's absurd I tell you. I have to make a stand.'

Flynn resisted the temptation to praise the nobility of his position. He felt sick. So far, no more leads had presented themselves. The door-to-door inquiries were a bust. The description of the girl and the men suspected of taking her, had been circulated more widely, but no hotels had so far accepted the strange group. All that had happened were the usual calls from people who had nothing to offer, except a desire to waste police time. The situation was grim; they needed a break.

Then the shrill sound of the phone jolted Flynn from the cycle of despair that was building up within him.

Monk reacted immediately and grabbed the phone from his desk.

'Hello...hello, who is this?' he said urgently. Then he paused for a minute and then looked with a frown at Flynn. 'I'll hand you over to him.'

'Who's this,' said Flynn, into the mouthpiece.

'Daddy, it's me,' said Bobbie.

'What on earth...?' scowled Flynn.

'Hold it daddy, before you start, I have a lead.'

'What do you mean?'

'The big man that Mr Fogg identified. His name may be Renat. He's known as Renat the Russian. Do you know him?'

The name was familiar, but from what Flynn could remember, he was a lone, small-time hood for hire.

'How do you know this?' asked Flynn, his tone softening.

'It doesn't matter, daddy. Look, there's a big search going on for him, from unexpected sources. How are things at your end? Have the kidnappers called back yet? They must know by now that they have the wrong person.'

'We're waiting. Look, get off the line. I don't want to be talking to you while they're trying to get through. I'll let the boys at the precinct know. Good work, Bobbie. Thanks.'

Flynn set the phone down and looked at Monk.

'My daughter may have just found a lead. We have a possible name for one of the kidnappers.'

'Your daughter? But I thought she was just here to write a piece about my dad,' said Monk, baffled by the turn in events.

'You have a daughter, Mr Monk. Trust me, you'll learn. Look, I need to ring the precinct now. Maybe you can give Mr and Mrs Belmont the good news that we have a break in the case. It may not guarantee anything, but if this is the guy then we'll find him. Count on it.'

'I'll let him know now,' said Monk.

20

The sky was not the only thing beginning to darken around 4pm. Bugsy returned to the house in a foul mood. By now, the extent of their mistake was readily apparent. They had lifted the wrong girl. Weeks of planning had gone up in smoke. For Bugsy, it was a catastrophe and, as far as he was concerned, the blame lay at the door of one person.

The dumb Russian, Renat.

The only problem was, he had suggested using him in the first place. He burst through the door of the house and raged at Renat.

'You dumb mutt, it's the wrong girl.'

Renat could have told him that and Violet certainly had. Now half the city's police force was looking for someone who was big and looked Russian while the rest of the city were laughing at them. More problematically, how many big Russians were there working on the fringes of crime in the city? Not many, bet Bugsy. The phone rang in the house before Bugsy could truly let fly at the cretinous Cossack.

Bugsy picked it up and almost spat his hello.

'You idiot,' said a voice at the other end of the line. 'What have you done?'

Bugsy glared at Renat and replied, 'Renat lifted the wrong girl, it's not my fault.'

Renat listened and shifted uncomfortably in his seat.

'You picked Renat, I blame you,' said the voice. 'All that money I put into this plan and now you've gone and made a complete mess of things.'

'We can still get something for the girl. It may not be quarter of a mill, but Monk will pony up some money, won't he?'

'No, he won't. And we are not going to ask him to do it either. You are going to do exactly what I tell you; do you understand? Exactly. As. I. Say.' The last words were spat out with a venom that made Bugsy redden in embarrassment. It was as if the person on the end of the line was addressing a village idiot. This was not designed to make Bugsy feel any better about the situation and it worked a treat. Bugsy felty miserable, which was not something he appreciated. Anger began to stir in his soul.

Bugsy began to say something but was immediately shot down by the withering tone of the caller.

'No. You say nothing. You do as I tell you. Do. You. Understand?'

This tone was rapidly turning Bugsy's foul mood into something murderous.

'Yes,' he snarled.

'Good. You will take the girl and you will bring her to the following address and leave her there. Then you will disappear. Both of you. You will not hear from me again. You will speak nothing of this to anyone. You will forget this ever happened and hope to hell that the police, and the parents of this girl, just decide to accept that it was all one big mistake and decide to let bygones be bygones. Understood?'

'Yes,' said Bugsy, in a defeated voice. 'Where do we drop her?'

He wrote down the address, which was in another part of Central Park. Then the voice said, 'And go now. Right. Now.'

Then the line went dead.

Bugsy sighed and ran a hand through his hair. He sat down on a wooden chair. Then he looked up at the Russian, who stared back at him impassively.

'Go get the girl. Blindfold her.'

'What we do?' asked the Russian suspiciously.

'Return her. No money. No bonus. Nothing. Zip,' growled Bugsy. For a moment he considered the idea of going it alone. Of demanding a ransom of sorts, but he realised that this was fraught with danger now.

Renat rose to his feet and trooped over to the door. Oddly, he felt relief. The idea had not been one that he was keen on. But he had to eat and jobs had not been coming his way. Yes, if anything he felt glad that this experience was over with and even that his role in this had unwittingly turned out for the best. He unlocked the door and opened it.

That moment, where he felt almost like a contented cat, lasted seconds. It evaporated as he gazed into the bedroom where Violet had been dozing.

The room was empty, and like an ice box, courtesy of the open window through which the child had evidently escaped.

Violet Belmont felt rested and ready to execute the plan that had formed in her head an hour earlier when she had realised the window could open. Outside, the snow had ceased, but the cloudy sky, at that time in the afternoon, meant it was really quite dark outside.

It was time to go.

She wasn't about to sit by and remain at the mercy of her captors. No, this was not how she had been made. Life had never been easy for her. A mum and a dad who drank too much until one day her mum had died and her father decided he didn't need a daughter. Violet had tried running away and living on the street. That had lasted exactly one day before she was picked up and deposited back to her house. Her father's reaction had convinced the cop, who had brought her back, that maybe she would be better off elsewhere.

A year in the Roman Catholic Orphan Asylum and then, the miracle. She had been chosen by a childless couple to be a daughter. Not only that, but the couple were also rich. He was a lawyer, while she was a glamorous lady who ran a house which even had a housekeeper. It felt like a dream.

Dreams never last though. At some point, you must wake up and face the cold, harsh reality of the day.

Violet had heard the arrival of Bugsy and this immediately prompted her into action. In a few moments, she had raised the window and nimbly clambered through into the open air. It was cold but Violet didn't care. The spirit of rebellion, which coursed through her at the best of times, was like a tidal surge within her. She was excited, scared and with a heart that beat like a jackhammer.

Outside now, she surveyed her options. She was in an alleyway which led out to the road at the front of the house. She had two options: run away from the house in a direction which would avoid the front window or, riskier, pass directly by the front door and then head in the direction of the city, whose bright lights she could see ahead. A long way ahead.

There was a reason why Violet was queen of hide and seek. She used strategy. It was a risk, but she felt deep inside that it could pay dividends. She would pass by the house.

Walking.

Violet took a deep breath and began to walk. She kept an even pace and resisted the temptation to sprint, screaming past the house. Her chest was so tight she could barely breathe as she began to stroll past the front window. Eyes fixed firmly ahead; she walked forward. Each step was a torment. Her legs felt like they were wading through quicksand yet, somehow, she had managed to pass the house unseen.

A few more steps and before the dam burst, she broke into a run, then a sprint, fuelled more by fear than exhilaration. She was free for the moment, but obstacles lay ahead. The distance to the city and the cold were a problem. She could see clearly in which direction she had to go, but was it really sensible to walk all the way there? Furthermore, when they discovered she was missing, they would be looking for her.

Perhaps she could find a policeman, but one look at the area she was in and she knew there would not be many around. There were some people on the street and they glanced at her but said nothing. Part of her wanted to run up to them and say that she had been kidnapped, but she suspected that would earn a scolding rather than sympathy.

She marched ahead, her mind spinning with the options that faced her. One thing was clear, she had to get off the main road. She made a detour down one street then proceeded, in a zig-zag fashion, in the direction of the city. She had no idea where she was. The area was much like the one she had been born into, before her life had changed direction so dramatically. It was like where she had come from, but different too. It was further away from the city and while she had been out in the dark before, it was never so far away from where she lived.

The plain fact was, she was lost. The snow began to fall gently on her. Without a coat, it would soon soak through. The elation that she had felt was slowly giving way to despair, the excitement had turned into fear.

She heard a voice behind her. An old man. He walked towards her and said, 'Hey kid. You want some candy?'

Violet didn't answer, she sprinted off before he had time to react. She ran for a couple of blocks, into an area where she could no longer see the city in the distance.

She looked around her and then up at the black, unforgiving sky. The snow fell on her, stinging her eyes or perhaps it was the tears. She wiped them away and walked forward, ignoring everyone ignoring her.

21

When she had finished speaking to her father, Bobbie was at a loss on what to do. She believed that she had made an enormous contribution to the case, but this was not enough. She wanted to be in on its conclusion. She had earned the right to do this. Even her father would see this... Or not.

Perhaps she was stretching credibility too far, but there was one other angle that could be of use. It was very much the last card that she would have wanted to play, but a story was a story. Hailing a cab, she gave an address for the one place she knew that reporters might not have considered going.

It was another expensive cab ride for Bobbie and gave her pause to consider whether or not she could actually afford her chosen career. She needed a raise, that was for sure. The thought of demanding it from that misogynistic bully, Thornton Kent, gave her some qualms. She needed to bring this story in for the paper. She needed another scoop that would trump what she had already achieved. Finding Renat the Russian was key.

The cab deposited her outside the Midtown North precinct where an old partner of her father worked. Bobbie was also aware that a certain detective Nolan worked there too. But he was more of an obstacle than anything else. She tried not to think of what "anything else" might mean in the context of the young detective.

One problem occurred to her as she entered the precinct. The captain at the precinct was a man she had only recently met and who was unlikely to view her with any favour. He had proved to be more of a hindrance than a help on a recent case, at new year and her father was a little suspicious of him.

The desk sergeant, a man named Moran, saluted Bobbie as she entered the building, 'Hi Red what brings you here? The old man ain't here if you're after him.'

Bobbie waved him away and laughed, 'Trying to avoid him actually.'

'Hey, if he's treatin' you bad, you just tell your Uncle Seamus.'

'He treats everyone bad,' pointed out Bobbie. 'Is Harry in?'

'Sure is. You know the way.'

Bobbie grinned at Moran and went through some double doors. She jogged up the stairs, passing a patrolman who was going to ask her where she thought she was going, but then left her as she seemed in a rush. She was.

Bobbie burst into the detective's office, causing several men to nearly spill their coffee. One of them was Sergeant Shane "Harry" Harrigan. Harrigan was on his feet in a moment and enveloped Bobbie in a bear hug, which had a few of the other men wondering if the way to a girl's heart involved possession of a beer belly and a fondness for muffins.

'Red, what the hell?' exclaimed Harrigan. This was his way of asking a number of things which ranged from how are you to why are you here? He frequently used this opaque line of questioning with criminal suspects, often to great effect. This was a source of mystery to his old friend and partner Inspector Flynn, but he could not argue with the results.

Bobbie, like most people, intuitively understood what was being asked and quickly got to the point. New York policemen were a busy breed of men. As much as she knew that he adored her and would be delighted that she had visited, it was not right for her to mess with his time. He had precious little of it usually.

'Look Harry, I need your help. It's the Violet Belmont kidnap case. I was there when it happened.'

'I'd have thought you'd have caught him by now,' joked Harrigan.

'I will,' grinned Bobbie. 'Look, can you check something for me?'

'Name it.'

'Mightn't be anything. Can you tell me what Hamilton Monk wrote in his suicide note? Someone must have a copy of it. Also, Renat the Russian, what can you tell me about him?'

Harrigan motioned for Bobbie to follow him to his desk. Sitting on it was a file which he handed to Bobbie.

'Don't tell your dad I showed you this,' said Harrigan in a low voice. 'Give me a minute or two while I make some calls.' The big detective picked up the phone while Bobbie glanced at the file he'd handed to her.

Renat the Russian was connected to a number of criminal gangs but appeared to be independent. He had no prison record but had been arrested on several occasions for intimidation or actual bodily harm. There was no mention of abduction in his record. In each case, the witnesses had retracted their stories and he had gone free. Obviously, he had powerful friends. She looked at the case report on his most recent misdemeanour. The victim had claimed, then retracted, a statement that said Renat had threatened him over an unpaid gambling debt. His lawyer was a man named Marcus Fisher.

Bobbie looked at a couple of the other incidents. On each occasion, Fisher had been the man to have him freed. She looked over at Harrigan who was on the phone. He was scribbling on a notepad. He waved her over. Harrigan put the phone down as Bobbie perched on his desk.

'What have you got, Harry?' asked Bobbie.

'I won't ask you to read my writing,' laughed Harrigan. 'He wrote as follows: *Last night I tried to kill Marjorie. It was too much to see her like this. She would not have wanted what has happened to her. Had she had her mind, she would have begged me to end her life. She has no life now. I could not do it. I could not hurt her. She was the love of my life, and she doesn't know me now. This is easier. I'm sorry to all of you. I can't bear it any longer.*'

Harrigan looked up when he had finished.

'Gosh,' said Bobbie. She felt a little emotional after hearing the note.

'He sure must have loved that lady,' said Harrigan.

Bobbie nodded. There was no question that the idea of a murder disguised as a suicide was now busted apart. This seemed too real. Too true to what she'd heard from the people near to Monk. The note had saddened her but, perhaps, the realisation too that she had nothing to go on now was the real blow.

'Was it handwritten?' asked Bobbie.

'Yes,' confirmed Harrigan.

So that was it. They would have checked the handwriting and it would confirm that Hamilton Monk had written the note. It meant she had nothing. No theory, no story and no next steps for finding the little girl. That was in the hands of the police and, bizarrely, a crime boss, Arnold Rothstein. Her role in this gave her some comfort, but she would like to have put a ribbon on the whole case by finding Violet. Bobbie handed the file back to Harrigan.

'Do you know this guy?'

Harrigan shook his head.

'Small time,' replied the big detective. 'The gangs bring in guys like this when they want to keep their hands clean.'

'You don't think it was a gang that did the kidnapping?' asked Bobbie, sitting up suddenly.

Harrigan laughed at this and replied, 'Not really their style and they probably wouldn't use this guy. He's strictly strong-arm. Good for threatening debtors, but not much more than that.'

'I see,' said Bobbie glumly. Then she tapped the file and said, 'He always gets sprung, though.'

'They do that. If you work for a gang they'll look after you. They get you a lawyer or, if you get put in the can, look after your lady or kids. It's part of the contract. Not that anything is written down. Keeps people loyal. Quiet.'

'I see. Marcus Fisher. Name seems familiar,' mused Bobbie. Then she shook her head. 'Maybe dad mentioned him.'

'Fisher does a lot of work for these people. Young guy, but tricky. I haven't come across him myself. I think O'Riordan and he have had a few barneys though.'

There was nothing else in there for Bobbie, so she thanked Harrigan and stood up from the table. Just as she did so, a familiar figure entered the detective's office. He stopped and stared at Bobbie.

'Detective Nolan,' said Bobbie trying not to sound too excited, or guilty. She couldn't decide which at that moment.

Nolan frowned from beneath a hat dripping melted snow onto the table. He set the hat on a desk and walked over to Bobbie and Harrigan.

'Solved the case?'

This brought a snort of laughter from Harrigan, who chuckled, 'I already asked that.'

Bobbie bristled at the young detective. Her eyes narrowed and she said, 'It's thanks to me you're looking for the Russian.'

'So I heard, Miss Flynn,' replied Nolan with just a hint of a smile. He nodded to her and for once this seemed a genuine acknowledgement. 'Good work.'

It wasn't quite a bottle of champagne being cracked open, those days were gone, but Bobbie tried not to think about how delighted she felt, by this hard-won compliment from Nolan.

'Have we heard anything more from the kidnapper?' asked Bobbie. Nolan shook his head before sitting down at his desk. Although she had never encountered such an extraordinary situation in her young life, Bobbie was confused by this and said so. 'I would have thought they would have been in contact to arrange something by now. They must know that they have the wrong girl.'

Nolan nodded at this, 'Yes, I've been wondering that myself.'

'Has my father sent you back to follow up on the Russian?'

'Yes,' said Nolan, glancing over towards Harrigan. 'Anything new, Harry?'

'No.' said Harrigan. 'I hear we're not the only ones looking for him either.'

'What do you mean?' asked Nolan.

'It seems he's upset the wrong folk with this.'

Nolan frowned before asking, 'How do they know we're after him. That was quick.'

Bobbie shifted, uncomfortably, from her perched position on Nolan's desk. Nolan spied this and fixed her with a steely gaze.

'Do you know why?'

Bobbie shrugged. Although she was not beyond telling an outright lie when the occasion demanded, which was often, something was preventing her doing so with Nolan. A shrug seemed as good a way as any of escaping further inquiry. Nolan stared at her for a moment, a frown creased his forehead.

'What does the inspector want you to do?' asked Harrigan.

Before Nolan could answer, a thought struck Bobbie and she stood up from the desk. The two detectives turned to her. Something on her face stopped them from saying anything. Both were curious.

'The kidnappers phoned Monk,' said Bobbie suddenly. She turned to Nolan and asked, 'Did they use a payphone?'

Nolan was shocked by the sudden switch in topic. He thought for a moment and then said, 'That's a good point. I didn't take the call, but we can easily find out.'

Bobbie was excited by what was on her mind.

'Don't you see, if they used a house phone, we could maybe trace the call.'

'That would take too long, Red,' pointed out Harrigan.

Bobbie shook her head, 'That's not what I mean. You've not found anyone answering their description at hotels or motels. Look, what if the kidnappers have rented a place for a few weeks. Perhaps they've had a phone installed. If we could find out who has had a phone installed in the last month then...'

'It could be thousands of people,' said Harrigan.

'And maybe they took a place because it already had a phone,' pointed out Nolan. His tone was not dismissive. If anything, he was trying to let Bobbie down lightly.

Bobbie slumped down on the desk again, 'You're right, I hadn't thought of that.' Another thought occurred to her, 'Has anyone mentioned seeing Renat with another man. Do we have a name for him yet?'

'No,' confirmed Harrigan, 'but we're following up. Renat is a pretty solitary character.'

'Not so solitary if he can afford to have a lawyer like the one you mentioned,' laughed Bobbie. Her mind was in a whirl, though. Something on her face must have betrayed her frustration. Even Nolan was curious as to what was on her mind.

'You look like you have wind,' said the sympathetic young detective. This brought a roar of laughter from Harrigan and a couple of the other detectives in the office. Even Bobbie laughed at this. She shook her head. There was something that was nagging her. When this happened, it was usually important and, when viewed in hindsight, obvious. They were missing an obvious piece of the jigsaw.

And then it hit her.

She shook her head and looked with wide eyes towards Nolan.

'You're not going to believe this. I'm not sure I believe it myself. It's incredible,' whispered Bobbie.

22

Right at that moment, Bugsy McDaid felt like howling. He and the big lug he'd drafted in to help them were in big trouble. It's difficult to drop an abducted child back to somewhere near her parents' home, when said abducted child, or the spawn of Satan, as Bugsy now considered her, had absconded through a window that neither he nor Renat had checked could be opened.

It didn't matter from which direction you looked at it, they had made the almightiest foul up. How their sponsor would react, he did not know. They'd never met. At least, not face to face. Communications had always been written. It seemed unreal. The money was real enough. Then finding out that this mystery person had rented a house, with a telephone, for a month was also a sign that they were serious people.

Now they had no child and no idea where the little imp had disappeared to. Bugsy had been driving around, looking, for close on an hour and still no sign of her. He was getting more and more nervous as the time passed and not just for the fact that they had no kid. The car he was using was stolen. At some point a cop might see him and the car then the game really was up.

It was never meant to be this way. They'll pay up, he'd been told. Grab the kid, take her to the house and lie low for a day. Return her the next day for the drop off at Penn Station. That was the plan. He and Renat had the whole exchange rehearsed. Bugsy would bump into Monk and put a gun to his ribs. The package would be deposited at a pre-arranged spot between Renat and Bugsy, then Monk would be told where to find the kid.

It seemed so easy and, as the station would be too crowded by office workers, there was no way the police would be able to keep track of the exchange.

Bugsy had found out what military tacticians had long known: no plan survives contact with reality. But reality had always been a hostile environment for people like him. It cast its shadow over his life and he knew he would never escape the continued sense of foreboding, of fear, and of failure.

He was now in the car, driving who knows where. He smacked the dashboard in frustration. The whole exercise was pointless. He knew that he would never find her. He pulled over to the side of the road and considered his options.

There were none. In fact, there were not even as many as that. The girl was lost, that much was obvious. Renat would never find her. If he did then he had instructions to take her to the drop off point at the Metropolitan Museum of Art. Even if he did produce the most unlikely miracle and do all that, neither he nor Renat would be paid. If anything, there would be someone out to get them.

All in all, the future looked bleak. Perhaps one thing was open to him, and he decided there and then to act on instinct. And the prime instinct, of all mankind, is first and foremost, survival.

He pulled out onto the road and then turned the car in the opposite direction to where he had been driving. Night had fallen now and perhaps, under cover of the darkness, he would fly away to freedom. In this case, freedom meant Philadelphia. He had a brother there. He could lie low for a while. Maybe even stay there.

But no plan survives contact with reality.

Little Violet Belmont would heartily have agreed with this sentiment just then. It was night and the streets glistened with the snow piled up on the sidewalk and the road. She walked an endless street, sometimes running when she didn't like the faces of the men looking at her strangely. She'd long since learned to take care of herself in this regard.

She forged on, utterly lost but with some sense that she was heading in the right direction. Every so often she would see the lights of Manhattan ahead of her, but then they would disappear again.

She was hungry, tired and thoroughly miserable. Worse, her dress was soaked through and she was shivering violently. She knew she needed shelter but there was nowhere she could trust to stay long enough without being accosted by someone she did not like the look of.

After what had seemed like an eternity walking, she finally reached a stretch of road where there were small stores. Most of them were hardware, but one offered possibilities. There were tables outside with fruit and vegetables laid out. Piles of it, in fact. Violet approached it. It occurred to her to go inside and tell them everything that had happened, but as she reached the door, she heard a couple arguing. They were standing behind the counter. The language was ugly and reminded her of her own father and mother, before her mother had died and she'd been moved to the orphanage.

Turning away from the door she reached over to the table and grabbed a couple of apples. This wasn't the first time she had resorted to stealing some food. A shout distracted her. She glanced inside the window and saw that the man had spotted her. He lifted the counter. Violet did not wait. She sprinted away from the shop and did not turn her head as she heard the man shout abuse towards her.

Violet kept running until she reached a street with built up apartment blocks. It was a dark, narrow street stretching like a forgotten artery through the decaying heart of the city. A feeble glow flickered from one of the streetlights until it died, leaving the street in darkness.

The silence was punctuated by the occasional drip-drip of water from a leaky drainpipe and a distant wail of a police siren. Perhaps they were looking for her. They would never find her here. The world had forgotten this street, this part of town and Violet couldn't blame it.

Turning back was impossible as she risked passing the store from which she had lifted the apples. A dog appeared out of nowhere and growled at her. Violet crossed the street. Like everything on this street, the dog seemed like it had been abandoned to its fate. Further up the street, she saw two men smoking cigarettes. They were sitting on the steps that led up to a house with boarded windows. Violet glanced to her right and thought about crossing the street, but the dog was tracking along in parallel on the other sidewalk. She pressed on regardless.

As she neared the men, they turned to look at her.

'Who are you, kid?' asked the man standing. His face was shaded slightly by his baker boy hat. The scar wasn't though. It ran along down from his cheek to his jaw.

'Violet,' answered the young girl, but she kept walking.

The man stood in front of her and blocked her passage.

'Where do you think you're going?' asked the man. The other man who was sitting laughed at this. Then he said, 'Leave her Joe.'

The standing man was not listening. He bent down slightly and said in a low voice, 'Did your mom and dad tell you not to speak to strangers?'

Violet stopped. She looked up at the man and nodded. Her heart was beating fast once more and she shivered, more because she was cold than afraid. And she was afraid.

The man laughed, 'You see that. Kid's scared, Al. Why you scared, kid? I'm a nice guy,' said the man she knew was called Joe.

'Wise guy more like,' said Al, standing up and drawing closer to Violet.

Joe grabbed her arm. 'I'm talking to you kid. Cat got your tongue. It's not nice to ignore adults when they're talking to you. Violet, you say? Like that kid that got nabbed?'

Violet tried to shake the man's hand off her arm, but the grip was tight. He was not quite hurting her, but his hand was clammy and she didn't like what was happening one bit. She wanted to cry but the tears had stopped coming years ago.

'Leave me alone,' said Violet, finding her voice at last. She tried shaking Joe's hand off, but the grip became stronger and this time it was hurting her. She knew all about this. Her father: her real father had been a bully. A drunken, no good, bully. Now the fear was being replaced by something else.

Anger.

Violet had taken just about everything she was going to take today.

'Let go,' she roared into the face of the man.

Joe exploded into laughter as did his friend Al. Violet could smell the drink off him. She knew that smell. Her father and mother had both spent more time drinking than parenting.

The grip grew tighter. Now it really was hurting her.

Violet had been here before. She was not quite eleven years old, but she knew how to deal with bullies.

She kicked Joe in the shin with the toe of her shoe.

Joe let out a howl of pain and immediately let go of Violet. This was her cue to escape. She took off. Joe was shouting a series of oaths while Al slapped his thigh and laughed at his friend's humiliation.

It was this, as much as anything, that made Joe's anger become a red-hot rage. He snarled a few well-chosen words at his pal and then spun around angrily. He saw Violet running down the street. Little did the girl know that she was running towards a dead end. Everything about this street was dead end and she was about to find this out.

Joe set off after her spurred on by the two foes that had followed him his whole life, anger and shame.

He caught up with Violet in a matter of seconds and grabbed her arm. He flung her down to the ground and stood menacingly over her. The laughter of his friend echoed down the street. It acted as an invitation to extract revenge on the little girl who had embarrassed him so.

'You think this is funny?' he hissed at Violet, who plainly thought nothing of the sort.

Violet felt real fear now. She had been beaten before. It's why they took her away from that house and put her in the orphanage. She steeled herself for what was to come.

Behind Joe, she heard a car screeching to a halt, but her eyes were on the man above her. And Joe's eyes were on her.

'Hey,' said a deep voice, from behind Joe.

This stopped Joe for a moment and he turned around. Even Violet's attention was diverted by the new arrival.

A yellow cab had pulled up across the road. From the cab stepped a man. A big man. He was not one for words. He was not one for thinking too hard about things. He just took orders. And his orders had been to find the girl.

He'd found her now.

Violet looked from the man who had been about to beat her, to the big Russian, who had abducted her.

Could this day get any worse she thought?

23

Every so often, as Nolan drove the car, he stole a glance at his attractive passenger and wondered, once more, if he was bringing her along for the right reasons. He was too good a policeman not to be able to know the look, the sound and the smell of a lie when he was in its presence. Perhaps it's because her dad was the legendary Inspector Flynn, the man that every senior cop he had encountered, said he should try to emulate. But that would have been a lie too. He consoled himself with the thought that if the old man did tear a strip off him for including her in an interview, he could say that it was her idea.

And it was *her* idea.

Worse, it had actually been something that they had all missed. Until she had seen what was so obvious. Whatever the old man might say, he could not avoid the conclusion that Nolan had already arrived at. Bobbie was more than a chip off the old block. He glanced at her again. She looked nothing like her dad, but according to Harrigan, Bobbie's mother had been quite a looker. Harrigan laughed affectionately at the idea of how Flynn could punch above his weight to catch her then he would catch himself and fall silent at her memory.

'You're quiet,' said Bobbie who had been completely aware, as women always are, of when men are stealing glances in their direction.

'Just wondering what I'm going to tell your dad, when he finds out that I've taken you along to this interview.'

Bobbie kept her eyes on the road ahead, but she grinned. Even from where he was sitting, he could see how they glittered with excitement. She had nice eyes. Wide set, greenish tinge and sparkling with intelligence. And fun. He wondered, not for the first time, what man was staring into those eyes.

They had first met only a few days ago when he had joined her father to investigate a murder at a party both she and her father had been attending. Now, just days later, they had been thrown together again. Another case.

'I think my dad knows what I'm like,' countered Bobbie. 'If he says anything, just tell me.'

It was interesting that she didn't point out that the trip downtown was due to what she had seen. This unaccountably pleased him as he felt a little embarrassed that she had made *another* breakthrough.

The offices of Belmont, Belmont & Fisher were located at the southern tip of Central Park. It was an old building by the standards of Manhattan, perhaps built sixty years ago. They were gradually knocking these down now and replacing them with buildings that stretched ever higher into the sky. Where would the high-rise buildings stop, he wondered. The clouds?

'Here we are,' said Nolan, pulling over to the kerb. A traffic officer frowned at them but could do nothing as they were in a police car.

They stepped out of the car and onto the sidewalk. Nolan went towards the traffic cop and was about to apologise to him, for parking on the street, when he said, 'Is that you Red?'

'Hello, Mickey,' said Bobbie to the cop.

'How's the old man?' asked the cop, that Nolan now knew was called Mickey.

'Grumpy as ever,' said Bobbie with a grin. 'You don't mind if we leave the car here?'

'No, you go right ahead,' said Mickey.

Nolan nodded to the cop who gave him a look that a suspicious uncle would give to his niece's prom date. As they entered the building, he said, 'Is there any cop you don't know?'

Bobbie glanced sideways at him and replied, 'Just that new kid Nolan.'

Nolan resisted smiling at this which only amused Bobbie more. They entered into the lobby of the building and made for the reception desk.

'We'd like to see Mr Fisher,' announced Nolan, flashing identification at the young woman behind the desk. She was attractive, if rather addicted to warpaint, in Bobbie's view.

'Third floor, officer,' said the young woman smiling up at the detective. The smile left her face when she glanced towards Bobbie.

They went to the elevator which took them up to the third floor. Two minutes later they entered the offices of Belmont, Belmont & Fisher. Bobbie had not had cause to visit many lawyers in the past, but she was rather disappointed by what she saw. The office building was old on the outside and the interior was not much better.

Nolan pushed through the double doors, with the name of the firm painted on the front. It was notable that "& Fisher" had been painted a little more recently than the father of Violet. Bobbie noted that Nolan had spent a moment looking at this. She wondered what he made of it. Then she wondered what she was supposed to make of it.

The woman at the reception was distinctly older that the one downstairs and, clearly, doubled as a secretary in the firm. She looked up over a half-moon *pince nez,* that was perched, dangerously, on an aquiline nose. She attempted a smile before giving up. Clearly her abilities were in words per minute, rather than a welcoming disposition.

'How can I help you?' she asked in a husky voice that suggested she had chain-smoked since first grade at school. The nearer Bobbie got to her, the more overpowering the smell of tobacco.

'We'd like to see Mr Fisher,' said Nolan to the woman whose name appeared to be Betsy.

'Have you an appointment?' asked Betsy, glancing towards a book just in front of her.

Nolan held up his identification and said, 'We'd like to see him now.'

This seemed to work. At least, it made Betsy shrug and she rose from her seat and went to a door which had Marcus L. Fisher on a shiny brass plate.

Marcus Fisher was justly proud of his rise to partnership in a middling Manhattan law firm. Often, he would pat his expanding waistline as if congratulating himself on an achievement that few in his graduating year had yet managed. It was different when you did not go to Harvard, or Yale, or Princeton. You actually had to be good at your job.

He glanced up at Betsy as she entered the office, trailing an air of burnt charcoal with her. Perhaps Belmont will see sense and try and get the young receptionist to replace this woman, thought Fisher. She was the very worst imaginable secretary to have. You needed someone conveying youthful vitality and efficiency. Betsy communicated decay and something ineffably staid. He'd speak to Belmont about it one day. The man would have to see sense. Betsy was not very enamoured with Fisher either. What he lacked in good manners he compensated for in smugness. The combination was not altogether one that appealed to her.

'Mr Fisher, there is a policeman here to see you, and a young woman,' said Betsy, in a voice that seemed to be gasping for air, following her pilgrimage from the front desk to the office, which was all of ten feet away.

Fisher was surprised by this. The terrible news about Belmont's awful daughter had come as a shock, of course, but why the police should want to see him was perplexing. Shouldn't they be out trying to catch the perpetrators of this deed? His sympathies were more with the abductors than the abducted. Violet Belmont did not like him and he certainly had no time for her. Quite what had made Belmont want to foster and possibly adopt the hell child, who came from the most degraded circumstances, was beyond him. Still, it was clearly a trying time for them. Belmont sounded on the edge of a nervous breakdown when they spoke earlier.

'Send them in,' said Fisher, as it occurred to him that the old hag had mentioned a young woman. Was the NYPD really hiring women now. They had the vote now, what else did they want?

When Bobbie entered the office, Fisher was on his feet in a moment, ready to man the barricades of the women's suffragette movement.

'I must say, I heartily approve of the NYPD's move to bring in women. Not before time,' lied Fisher, with a smile so insincere that even he wondered if he'd pushed things too far. He noted the rather surprised reaction of the two new arrivals to his welcome and decided to calm himself down a little. Fisher glanced at Nolan. Good-looking, certainly, but the suit was cheap, and he probably had a thick Bronx accent.

'Good afternoon, Mr Fisher, thank you for seeing us on such short notice,' said Nolan, instantly dispelling Fisher's illusion about his accent. While the accent wasn't Ivy League, it certainly wasn't downtown either.

'It would be my pleasure,' said Fisher, making sure to catch the young woman's eye. Smoothly done, he thought. He stretched his arm out, to indicate that they could take a seat.

Betsy, who was hovering at the door, was about to leave when she heard Fisher say, 'Can my secretary get you a coffee?' Betsy shot him a look that would have withered a cactus. He didn't see it, as his attention was completely absorbed by the radiant presence of the young woman, he thought was a detective. Bobbie wondered when Nolan would step in and point out that she was a journalist.

He didn't.

Instead, he went straight to business.

'No need for coffee. Mr Fisher, we are investigating the kidnapping of Miss Violet Belmont. One of our avenues is the possibility that one of your clients may be connected with the abduction.'

This was not good news. Fisher was aware that one of the reasons he had been given a partnership with Belmont was that he had brought quite an extensive client list to add to Belmont's. The firm had been in the hands of Belmont's father, and now that he had retired, the son was slowly running it into the ground. He was a smart man, no question, but he could not "sell" either himself or the firm to prospective clients. That was why he had brought in Fisher and made him a partner.

It was a good match. Belmont & Belmont had been an old firm with a decent reputation, but clients who were aging or dying off. They, specifically, Fitzroy, had singularly failed to bring in new blood. The children of their original clients were going elsewhere. He, Marcus Fisher, on the other hand, had single-handedly helped turn the firm's fortunes around. This was thanks not just to his gregarious nature, but also due to a charming lack of scruples when it came to choosing his clients.

His reasoning was sound.

The clients most in need of help were the ones who danced closest to the edge of legality or simply leapt into the abyss with nary a care. Marcus Fisher was considered a safe pair of hands, by more than one criminal gang, who might need his services. So far, his involvement was strictly with the lower echelons of the criminal fraternity, but this was merely a period where he earned his spurs. Soon the bigger boys would come calling, he hoped, as trust was earned.

'You don't say,' said Fisher, trying to show genuine concern.

Nolan did not feel like repeating himself, so he pressed on with the key question. He said, 'Renat Murdrych has been identified as one of two men, possibly connected to this deed. Where can we find him? We have an address, but it seems he has left this recently. So we need to know what you have on file.'

Bobbie chimed in at this point, not wholly unaware that Fisher was trying to impress her.

'And could you let us know the names of other recent clients you have helped spring from jail, as this may help us find the other kidnapper,' asked Bobbie.

Nolan glanced wryly at Bobbie, which made her feel rather pleased that her question had impressed him and irritated that she was rather pleased that it had impressed him. Had Nolan been aware of the train of thought speeding, in a runaway fashion, through her head, he might have considered the very real truth that men simply cannot win.

'You're sure it's Renat? I mean he has had his occasional misunderstanding with New York's finest, but he's not a bad man.'

Oddly, Fisher meant it and there was something in his confusion which for a moment made Bobbie and Nolan wonder if they had made a mistake.

'We are not sure, Mr Fisher, but we certainly would like to meet him and either strike him off our list or get any information on who he might consort with.'

Fisher rose from his desk and went towards a large wooden filing cabinet. He said, 'Fair enough. Well, anything to help Fitzroy and Olivia. They're in such distress over this whole thing.' He opened one of the drawers and leafed through a few files until he found the one he wanted. He opened it up and said, 'The address I have is West 49th Street in Hell's Kitchen.'

Nolan frowned. This was the same as the police had. He shook his head.

'Nothing else?' he asked sullenly.

'No.'

'Associates?'

'I'm sorry, I just can't say,' said Fisher.

'Can't say or won't say?'

'A little of both,' admitted Fisher. 'Client confidentiality is very important to me.' He looked towards Bobbie as he said this, to impress upon her that he was a man of the utmost integrity. To Bobbie's eyes he even appeared to stand up a little straighter and pull in his stomach.

'Can you tell us who else you have represented in the last two months with the police,' asked Bobbie.

Fisher thought for a second and then decided that this was a reasonable request and one they would be able to find out anyway.

'Just three other people.'

'Who are they?' asked Nolan.

'Ray Donatello.'

'Where can I find him?' asked Nolan, pen poised over his notepad.

'Sing Sing,' said Fisher self-consciously. He hated failing his clients even when they were as guilty as Donatello had been. 'He's doing thirty for manslaughter. Then there's Frederick Fulton.'

'Freddie the forger?' asked Nolan.

'The same,' confirmed Fisher.

'We can strike him off our list,' said Nolan, grimly.

'Why,' chimed Bobbie.

'He was killed outside a speakeasy a few weeks before Christmas,' said Nolan. 'Probably upset someone he shouldn't have.'

'And the other?' asked Bobbie, trying to hide her disappointment.

'That would be Benjamin McDaid', said Fisher. 'He goes by the name Bugsy.'

24

Joe heard the voice from the cab and looked up. The cab door opened and out stepped Renat. While Joe was no coward, he was no fool either. One look at Renat told him that this was someone you only argued with if you were holding a Roscoe. He was not in possession of such an important piece of hardware and therefore was enormously less inclined to pick a fight.

'What do you want?' asked Joe, still holding onto Violet who had stopped squirming, less out of fear than of genuine curiosity as to what was going to happen next. She'd seen men fight before. It was ugly and fascinating in equal measure. Something about her Russian kidnapper suggested that he would not break sweat with the latest adult to spoil her day.

'Girl,' said the loquacious Russian, pointing to Violet.

Joe sneered at this, 'A little young for you, don't you think?'

Al was standing beside Joe now but had also marked out his escape route as Renat loomed ever closer. His size was a consideration. And that consideration was: how fast can he run? The cab behind Renat tore off as the driver had quickly sized up the situation and decided that he was no hero.

Joe had by now decided it was time to free his hand from the wriggling imp. He threw her to the ground, like a rag doll and extracted a flick knife from his pocket. Seeing Joe do this made Al do likewise, although he had little intention of putting it to any use. The Russian was enormous.

It would be like attacking a wall with a toothpick.

Violet got to her feet and considered running off, but there was something horribly compelling about seeing the giant Russian facing off against the two louts who'd grabbed her.

Renat stopped and stood in the middle of the road. He pointed to Violet.

'Come,' he said, gesturing with his hand.

Joe moved between Violet and the Russian. Al moved around to the Russian's right. This was less a flanking attack manoeuvre than a desire to ensure his escape route was not in the direction Violet had discovered was a dead end. He waved his knife around in a manner that Renat immediately identified as rank amateur. Even Joe glanced in the direction of his friend and saw the knife being waved around like it was being used to fend off an invisible wasp.

The situation was now something of a stand-off. Neither Joe nor Al was remotely interested in making the first move. In fact, Joe was secretly regretting the whole thing. Closer inspection of the Russian's face only consolidated the impression given by his bulk that this was a man wholly comfortable with violence. It was one thing to mug someone at night, and Joe had done that so many times, it was quite another to tangle with a man that looked like he would pound Jess Willard to a pulp.

Violet sized up the situation in an instant. She did not have a knife, but her next words cut so much deeper.

'Not so brave now, are you, Joe?' she sneered. She had decided, all things considered, better the devil you know. Had it been the one called Bugsy, she might have hedged a little.

Joe was never happy being mocked. It was even more humiliating when the source of the abuse was a ten-year-old she-devil. But Violet hadn't quite finished yet. Her assessment of the state of play was uncannily acute.

Much to Renat's dismay and Joe's horror, she stepped forward towards the knife-wielding bully. She stared at him for a moment. He stared back at her.

Then she stuck her tongue out.

Joe was too shocked to comment on this development, as indeed was Al. The two simply looked on as Violet turned tail and walked towards the Russian, with a jaunty wave of the hand and a dismissive, 'So long, losers.'

Renat, under normal circumstances, would have made sure the little girl crossed the road safely, but it was best to keep an eye on the two men with the knives. He backed away from them while Violet continued over to the other side and headed back down the street towards the main road.

The two men, meanwhile, finally recovered their senses. Joe started towards the Russian, but without any earthly intention of engaging him. Every step was a prayer that the big man would not call his bluff.

Renat was caught between delivering some instantaneous justice or keeping an eye on his young charge. He stopped.

Joe stopped.

Renat pointed at him and then waved his index finger in a manner that was universally understood to mean "don't-even-think-about-it". Then, seeing the defeat in the Joe's eyes, Renat turned and followed Violet down the street.

'Are we going back to the house?' asked Violet.

'No. Home,' said Renat.

Violet stopped and stared up at her former captor.

'Home?'

'Museum,' repeated the Russian.

Not quite home, but she knew where they were headed, and it was near enough. This was a turn up and a welcome one at that. Violet nodded. Then she pointed to a car coming towards them. It was yellow.

'Look!' she exclaimed. 'A cab.'

'No money.'

Violet stopped and looked at the Russian. Then she turned and looked at Manhattan, a few miles in the distance. Renat shrugged. Then he pointed in the direction of the city.

'Walk.'

25

Bobbie and Nolan drove back towards midtown in silence. It was a comfortably uncomfortable silence. The one most married couples would recognise when one partner has been proven right and the other is waiting for an I-told-you-so. Of course, most men who value a peaceful life will studiously avoid seeking vindication. Life is too short, and a woman's memory is too long. Bobbie, however, decided against pointing out that she had been right. It's much more fun to hear it from the male you are with.

Nolan knew that it was incumbent upon him to issue this validation. The question he was deliberating, as they headed back to the precinct, was the extent of the praise. Should he go full bore and effusively congratulate Bobbie? No chance. He doubted Bobbie would much want that, as it would smack of mockery. Equally, a terse "well done" might suggest sour grapes. *And she had helped.* Nolan was convinced if this. He had to commit to saying something, though.

'Well done, Miss Flynn,' said Nolan glancing at his travelling companion. 'This is a useful lead.'

Perhaps, in time, such reserved praise might needle her but, right at that moment, coming from a man who she knew her father quite liked and who clearly had the respect of his colleagues at the precinct, nothing could have sounded sweeter. A warm glow permeated her body, and she smiled back at Nolan. The fact that the source of the praise was over six feet tall, with nice eyes and wavy black hair of course had absolutely no bearing whatsoever on her delighted reaction.

They arrived back at the precinct with the clock striking five. Bobbie had to run to keep up with the long strides of the young detective. By the time they were at the detectives' office, she was almost out of breath and the satisfaction of her contribution, as well as the praise earned, was rapidly diminishing.

Nolan burst through the office door causing the three men in the office to glance up sharply. Just as Nolan was about to update them on what they'd learned, Bobbie came in. Everyone's attention was diverted by her arrival.

Including the detective sitting in the office at the far end. This office belonged to Captain Francis O'Riordan. That's what the brass plate said on the door. He'd bought it the day he was made captain. O'Riordan came stomping out of the office when he saw Bobbie. He was a large man, around Nolan's height, but much broader. His face looked like it had been squashed into a square head a little too small to contain it fully. His neck had not been seen in at least a decade if it had ever been seen at all. To round off a less than matinee idol appearance, he had a shock of red hair which stood up on end, as if he had seen the ghost of the first man he'd killed in the line of duty. When he frowned, his jowly face resembled nothing less than a constipated bulldog.

And he was frowning now.

Fixing his eyes on Bobbie, and pointing a large paw at her, he said something resembling, 'What is she doing here?' This was what Nolan interpreted from the litany of swear words that were transmitted between teeth which already had a cigar to deal with.

Nolan hadn't a lot of time for O'Riordan, and the feeling was certainly mutual. Bobbie, who had met the captain on New Year's Eve when he had arrested the wrong person, had even less time for the man. She found him repellent, and she knew her father had his suspicions about him.

Bobbie felt for Nolan at this point. He was in a no-win situation. The truth was embarrassing, and it would not reflect well on Nolan or, indeed, the other men in the office if it were revealed that she had been instrumental in guiding the investigation. It was time to take matters in hand before they careered out of control.

'I was a witness to the kidnapping,' stated Bobbie confidently.

It would be fair to say a number of heads shot round to her at this.

'You saw who kidnapped the kid?' exclaimed O'Riordan in a manner that could not have been more sceptical than if Bobbie had proclaimed herself to be Babe Ruth in disguise.

'Yes. I was on my way to interview Jefferson Monk,' said Bobbie. This was true. 'I saw the two children,' she added, sticking to the truth like a novice ice skater to the side of the rink. 'I didn't get a good view of Renat the Russian or,' she paused at this point and glanced in the direction of Nolan. The detective nodded. Grimly, it must be said, but it was a nod, no question. Bobbie pressed on, 'Nor did I get a good view of Bugsy McDaid, but the old Englishman who was in the park did.'

'Bugsy McDaid,' said Harrigan, who had been listening in on the exchange. He had gone from very amused to intensely curious in the blink of an eye.

'Yes,' confirmed Nolan, giving Harrigan the eye. 'I, that is, we, believe that Renat's accomplice was Bugsy McDaid.'

'Doesn't sound like Bugsy's style,' said O'Riordan, unconvinced. That said, everything O'Riordan said sounded sceptical, with more than a spoonful of cynicism thrown in for good measure.

Nolan felt it was time to gain a greater foothold in the conversation lest it travel too far down the path of the fantasy embarked upon by Flynn's daughter.

'We have established,' said Nolan before adding, 'sir, that Renat the Russian and McDaid both have the same lawyer.'

'Who is?' asked O'Riordan, just a hint of doubt creeping in that the young detective might not be onto something.

'Marcus Fisher,' replied Nolan.

'Who is?' said O'Riordan before realising he remembered coming across someone called that before.

'That's Belmont's partner,' said Harrigan right on cue. The cue being Bobbie frowning towards him to get involved.

It was one thing to give Nolan a dose of contempt and credulity, but Harrigan was a different prospect for O'Riordan. Harrigan had been around the precinct since the stone age and was generally the most liked man in the building. The captain was not prepared to tangle with the sergeant and usually gave him plenty of slack.

'Good work, Harry,' said O'Riordan, turning to Harrigan as if he'd just made a wonderful connection.

'Well done, Harry,' said Nolan, a ghost of a smile on his lips and his eyes twinkling with mischief.

Harrigan was enjoying his moment in the sun shamelessly. He puffed out his chest and said with a grin, 'You can count on me.' This was directed at Nolan and Bobbie.

'Thataboy, Harry,' said Bobbie with a wide smile. 'Hey, Harry, can you let my pop know about McDaid. It'll help back at the house. You know, give a sense of momentum in the case.'

'Right on it, Red,' said Harrigan.

Nolan's eyes narrowed as he looked at Flynn's daughter. She caught the look and gave a half-smile of triumph back. Nolan nodded to her but said nothing. The immediate danger appeared to have passed for them both. However, it was only good sense to allow O'Riordan to think that he was in control of matters.

'Get a call out to uniform that we need to haul Bugsy in here pronto.'

'Yes sir,' said a detective who was halfway through a muffin. This was Detective Timothy L Yeats, a man for whom the euphemism "big boned" must surely have been created. He was around Nolan's height and about the same wide. His sterling career as a defensive tackle at college had come to an end when he picked up the quarterback and deposited him in the end zone. This might have been considered a rather unusual tactic at the best of times, but when it was his own quarterback, who he'd caught messing around with his girl, both the team and the college decided it was time they should go their separate ways.

The police welcomed him with open arms.

Yeats carried out O'Riordan's instruction with alacrity. Perhaps too much so, because it meant that the captain could now return his attention to the highly unwanted presence of

Inspector Flynn's daughter. Bobbie had been anticipating this and thinking furiously about how she could delay the impending dismissal.

Even Nolan was looking at her at this point and wondering what other card she had up her sleeve. He had to give her some credit, she had managed to stick around an investigation that, by rights, should have seen her exit stage left several hours ago. He found himself hoping that she would once more pull the proverbial rabbit from the cloche hat under which she hid her auburn hair.

Bobbie fixed Nolan with a "help-me-here" look, but the detective was fresh out of inspiration by this point. He sketched a subtle shrug and grimaced.

O'Riordan had the prey in his sights, and he stalked forward towards Bobbie, evil intent in his eyes. When he reached her, he removed the cigar from the side of his mouth. This was never a good sign.

Just as nemesis was about to strike, Bobbie heard the three words that every woman expects to hear, even on those rare occasions that she is wrong. These were the words denied to Napoleon when he pointed to the map and mused, 'What's Waterloo like?' or Caesar when Brutus casually suggested he join him and the boys down at the Forum to get ripped.

'Bobbie,' shouted Fleischer who had been manning the phone on another task related to the kidnapping.

All eyes, including O'Riordan's, turned to Fleischer.

'You were right,' he shouted.

26

Not much was going right for Inspector Flynn at the Monk household. Jefferson Monk remained resolute in his insistence that he would not pay the two-hundred-thousand-dollar ransom. Monk's wife was not speaking with her husband and Flynn was feeling the heat from both husband and wife for being partially to blame for this because they had not yet located the child. The news from the precinct, about the possible second kidnapper, was welcome and would provide some respite. But, they still could not be certain of any of this. In short, they had nothing. Only hypotheses.

Meanwhile, Fitzroy Belmont sat by the phone in Monk's office, waiting for the next call from the kidnappers, although for close on ten minutes he'd held the line up in a low-voiced conversation with his wife.

It was past five now and Flynn felt heartily sick of everyone and everything. His mood was not helped by the ghostly and sneering presence of the Beauregard siblings who were floating around like an odour you can't locate, at no one's insistence, to see what happened to a child they disliked and who disliked them in turn.

All in all, the atmosphere lacked a certain conviviality and, worst of all, Flynn wished he'd kept Bobbie in the house although, he had to concede, it sounded as if she was proving to be a great help in identifying the kidnappers. He could have done with hearing her voice, even her opinions which, notwithstanding his views on her ever becoming a crime reporter, he respected and valued. He'd let her leave the house because he knew the press pack would descend and, at least, she would have had a head start on the story.

The arrival of the evening paper confirmed this. The house received half a dozen of them. All led with the story of the kidnapping, but only one correctly identified the girl who had been abducted. It was splashed across the front page of the *New York American*

A LITTLE MISS TAKEN

Underneath the headline was the by-line – *by Robert Flynn, our eyewitness reporter on the scene.*

Well, you could not argue that the old detective had done well by his daughter, and it hurt. This would only fan the flames of her desire to become a crime reporter. He stood by the window and stared out at the snow, descending lazily onto the press pack assembled outside. No doubt they would be sharpening their quills to have a go at him. Without a major break in the case, and the perceived favouritism he'd shown to his daughter, they would be using him for target practice over the next few days, and that was before he contemplated the unthinkable, that anything would happen to the girl.

As he thought this, he scolded himself for succumbing momentarily to self-pity. The safe return of an innocent child was not just the most important consideration here, it was the only one.

Flynn stepped away from the window, headed out into the corridor and ran into Jefferson Monk's brother. A cigarette dangled precariously from his lower lip that might have made a young girl's heart a-flutter but only made Flynn want to swipe it away.

'Any news?' asked Quincy Monk.

Flynn shook his head. Harrigan had indicated that they were pursuing a few leads, particularly regarding the potential kidnappers, but the old detective was not prepared to show his hand in this regard, even if it was frustrating to the young man. For all he knew, this young man might be involved. Any of them might be.

Quincy didn't seem to care anyway. It was almost as if the question had been rhetorical. Flynn suspected he smelled drink on him but decided not to mention it. People dealt with things in different ways. And this was the very worst of situations.

'I'll let you know,' said Flynn.

The door to Monk's office opened. Fitzroy Belmont appeared. He slumped a little against the door frame. His eyes were bloodshot and his posture would have indicated a drunk to Flynn's eyes. In fact, Flynn could see a bottle of whisky on the table by the phone. This wasn't the time or indeed the person to reprimand about flouting Prohibition, so he left it alone.

'No news from my guys,' said Flynn which was not quite the truth. He knew about the lead, regarding the rental properties, that they were investigating and also that Belmont's partner, Fisher, may have, unwittingly, been the conduit for the men that had kidnapped the child by mistake. This meant nothing without proof and they had exactly nothing. Only theories.

Belmont nodded lamely. He glanced at the newspaper headline and smiled mirthlessly.

'Surely they'll see that they've made a mistake.'

Flynn was not so sure. If they were stupid enough to lift the wrong girl, they might be stupid enough to disbelieve the overwhelming evidence.

'Why don't you go back to your house?' suggested Flynn. 'No point in waiting here for a call that may not come.'

Belmont shot Flynn a look, before replying in a resigned voice, 'You might be right.'

Augustus St Clair appeared from another room at this point. He walked over to the lawyer and placed a hand on his shoulder. There was nothing he could think to say, but the gesture was met with an appreciative nod from Belmont.

Flynn turned his attention to the tall banker and said, 'I was just saying to Mr Belmont that he should head back home and wait with his wife. There's nothing to be gained staying here now. The kidnappers will know they have the wrong girl.'

'They must give her back, Inspector Flynn. What can they possibly gain now?' said St Clair.

'Yes, I agree,' said Flynn, trying to sound upbeat. Oddly, having heard who was responsible, he felt better about Violet Belmont's prospects. If it really was Renat the Russian and Bugsy McDaid, then the chances were better now. Neither man had been implicated in murder. They were strictly low-level hoodlums. Murder was not their style; they would become hunted mercilessly by police and the gangs they worked with.

'I'll get one of the men to take you,' offered Flynn.

'Thanks,' replied Belmont. He glanced towards Quincy. In his eyes was a question. It was met with an uncomfortable shake of the head. Quincy's eyes flicked towards the newspaper.

'They'll see sense. They have to,' said Quincy. He looked to St Clair then Flynn for support.

Flynn was not in the market for false hope, so he repeated his earlier suggestion, 'I'll get one of my men now.'

A few minutes later two policemen appeared at the door. They led the lawyer outside. The door closed and Flynn stood in the hallway and listened to the sound of shouting as Belmont walked towards the reporters.

'What do you think inspector? Has my brother condemned that little girl to death,' asked Quincy. Flynn looked at the young man. Quincy's face was desolate and weak in equal measure. A man who was a slave to pleasure. Spoiled beyond redemption.

Flynn had no answer to that question. He could only hope that his instincts regarding Bugsy and Renat were correct. The silence hung heavy between them and then it was shattered by the sound of the telephone in the hallway. Flynn's head shot around to the candlestick telephone which was almost shaking on the table. He grabbed the earpiece and put the microphone to his mouth.

'Hello, who is this?'

'Inspector,' said a familiar voice on the other end of the line. 'It's Harry. Your girl came up trumps again.'

27

'I'm hungry,' complained Violet. She could have added cold and very tired, but with adults, she'd noted, their sympathy levels declined, exponentially, as you added more complaints. Trial and error had told her that hunger was the one thing that usually delivered the best results, as it required that you stop and rest anyway.

Renat shot a glance in the direction of the little girl, and she was ridiculously little alongside him. She had been through a lot to give her some due, but what more could he do than bring her home. In this case home meant the agreed delivery place. He'd briefly considered returning to the rented house, but as Violet had made it halfway home it seemed they may as well walk the rest of the way.

'Why don't we take a cab?' asked Violet.

The big Russian shrugged and said again, 'No money.'

'My dad will pay when we get home.'

This was a good point and one that Renat had been wondering about himself and yet two things were stopping him from taking Violet up on this eminently sensible suggestion. One was self-preservation. He might drive himself all the way into a trap. The second thing was oddly more important now.

He'd found her just in time to save her from something that Renat did not want to think about, too closely. There were some bad people in this city, he thought, oblivious to how the good folk of New York might consider a kidnapper from Russia. In an odd way, the former sergeant in the White Army felt he now had a duty to return the child to her home safely. His conscience was clear on having abducted her in the first place. That was business. He would always have ensured there would have been a reunion between the kidnap victim and the ransom payer.

Business. Nothing else.

They were on Park Avenue, now having negotiated Third Avenue Bridge thanks to a free ride on a bus which they hopped on and off without paying. Violet had rather enjoyed that. So had Renat.

'How much further?' asked Violet.

'Mile,' said Renat although he had no earthly idea. He hadn't been in this part of town much. He knew Broadway and the surrounding area quite well. They were in Harlem now and he tended to stay away from this area unless he was being paid to go. Once he was earning money and he had a Roscoe in his pocket, he felt a little better about the world. He had neither just then. And he was feeling the pangs of hunger himself. The little imp had reminded him that he'd not eaten since this morning.

The gnawing emptiness in his stomach had been a constant companion for him back in Russia even when he had the farm. Until they took it from him. They took everything from him. Was it only four years ago? He thought of his field, his wife and the child she was carrying. It was the closest he'd come to having a dream for the future. The communists had taken them all from him. Tears stung his eyes.

They say revenge is a dish best served cold. This is true, but they don't tell you that the feeling is momentary. It's never enough to satisfy the cravings you feel. No amount of killing, and he had killed many, would ever bring back what he had lost.

'We're going to the Met?' asked Violet. She wanted to talk, if only to take her mind off the emptiness in her stomach.

'Museum.'

'The Met?' pressed Violet, wanting to be sure.

'Art,' replied Renat.

'The Met,' nodded the little girl.

Renat just nodded his head too. He wasn't sure himself. This seemed to satisfy Violet and they walked along an avenue that highlighted the extremes in wealth in the city. Park Avenue ran from the poorest part of Harlem to the very wealthiest part where the swells lived.

The redbrick buildings and the broken streetlamps gave the street a forbidding presence. Yet, it was familiar too. Even Violet sensed that Renat was walking a little more quickly.

At least the snow had stopped, but the chill Violet felt went right to her bones. She shivered as she dodged around ice patches on the sidewalk. They passed one group of men after another, standing on street corners or sitting on steps leading up to their homes. They all stopped talking and stared at the unlikely twosome.

Renat kept his eyes straight ahead, but Violet could not stop herself looking at the men she passed. They were people she recognised if not in person, then by type. Most were harmless, adapting themselves to the hostile, uncaring environment with native cunning. Among them were men who believed in adapting the world around them to their needs.

There was no morality here. While Violet may not have been able to articulate this, she certainly recognised it when she saw it.

Renat, she now knew, meant her no harm. She had perceived this early on. Since the moment he had effectively risked his life to protect her from the hoodlums. Perhaps even earlier. And now he was taking her home.

'Hey bud, got a light?' asked one man standing by a group. He spoke to Renat, but his eyes were on Violet.

'No,' said Renat walking past him, eyes straight ahead. Violet's eyes were on the man. It was a hard face, half-hidden beneath a baker boy hat that cast a shadow over his eyes leaving only the scowl to contemplate.

'I'm talkin' to you bud,' called the man as Renat went past.

Renat and Violet ignored him, but they could not disregard the sound of discontented murmurs and then the sound of bodies rising from the steps. Violet felt Renat grab her hand. He was keen to get away from the dark street to one up ahead that was well lit. It was fifty yards away. Renat sped up which forced Violet to do likewise. She didn't ask why. Her heart was in her mouth. Despite her tired limbs, she recognised the urgency.

Then they heard the men starting to run. Renat picked up Violet suddenly and started to run also. The Russian was no sprinter, but he was strong. Violet was no heavier to him than lifting a cat. She turned to their pursuers. They were ten yards away. She switched her attention to the main street. It was twenty yards away. One thought beamed around her head.

They wouldn't make it.

Renat had worked that out for himself. The purpose behind the sprint was to get a little closer to the light. At a certain point he slowed down and said, 'Run.'

He set the little girl down and pushed her ahead. Then he turned to face the four men who were running after them. Violet didn't turn around. She sprinted towards the street corner. Behind her she heard the shouting and grunting. The sound of violence. The sound of *men*.

She spun around and saw Renat grappling with two men. Two of the other men lay in a heap on the street. She stared at the sight of the big Russian being forced to the ground. He had no chance now and there was nothing she could do. Tears stung her eyes. She screamed. And screamed again. One word.

'Renat.'

28

'Where do you think you're going?' asked Nolan, as Bobbie fell in step alongside him.

'With you, Buster. I've earned it, don't you think?' responded Bobbie.

This was a moot point. Her instincts had certainly guided the investigation, perhaps even given it momentum. Nothing had been proved, though.

Yet.

O'Riordan, Harrigan and Fleischer had headed off towards the rented house that Harrigan had uncovered from Bobbie's suggestion. Meanwhile, Yeats and Nolan were to head to the address of the man who had signed the short-term tenancy of the house. Yeats was never going to say a word against Red, so it was left to Nolan to tell the daughter of Inspector Flynn that there was no way a young woman could accompany the police, as they undertook their duties. Especially not one who was connected to the press.

Yeats looked over at Nolan expectantly. In this case, expectantly took the form of a broad grin and a "not-my-problem" countenance.

Nolan shook his head and wrestled with the pros and cons of having the young woman tag along. His short experience with her was solidifying his view that she had a good head on her shoulders, a very good head in fact and was not prone to panic in a tight situation.

And this was the clincher.

Nolan still could not believe where they were going.

Yeats elected to drive while Nolan sat in the front with him. He ignored his colleague's persistent smile and instead chose to keep his eyes fixed firmly ahead. Bobbie, meanwhile, decided that she had made it this far, so silence was the best policy.

The hush in the car contrasted with the noise outside as cars slithered and sloshed along a road covered with blackened snow, beeping horns to warn foolhardy pedestrians of the peril they faced with the out-of-control automobiles.

The calm interior was fully at odds with the mood of both Bobbie and Nolan. Nature abhors a vacuum and where humankind is concerned, it's none too keen on quiet either. It gives you time to think. And both Bobbie and Nolan's thoughts were speeding along at a faster rate of knots than Yeats was permitting the car to go.

What if I'm wrong, thought Bobbie? Nolan was thinking along similar lines although his fear was having trusted the young woman's intuition too much. It may have scored a few bullseyes, but as any baseball coach would tell you – you're only as good as your last game.

And she had been wrong about the death of Hamilton Monk.

Or had she?

They would soon find out. Bobbie's sense of certainty was always tempered by the knowledge that she risked interpreting the evidence they had, with her growing belief that she knew what had happened. The temptation to ignore evidence that was inconsistent with her suspicions had to be avoided at all costs. Her father had taught her that, little suspecting the child he was helping with her history homework would, one day, use it for a cause he would heartily have disapproved of: a police investigation.

'This is fun,' said Yeats, staring at the road ahead. He might have been referring to the hazardous conditions or, and Nolan was fairly certain of this, he meant the muted atmosphere in the car.

Nolan grinned at his colleague. They were a similar age and had arrived in the precinct a few weeks apart. He liked Yeats. There was an honesty about him. The story of how he'd been kicked out of college had made him something of a legend among the men. They liked him. More importantly, they trusted him. He was not perhaps as gifted an investigator as Nolan, but he had other qualities that sometimes, make that often, came in useful when dealing with the seamier side of New York.

Up ahead they saw Central Park. They were nearing their destination. Returning to near the scene of the crime. Bobbie glanced out of the window and saw shoppers and office workers battling their way along the sidewalk. Christmas lights lit the way. They'd come down soon. Bobbie felt sad at this. She loved the holidays, but without her mom it was not quite the same.

She glanced away from the scene outside and found Nolan looking at her from the front passenger seat. She wondered what he thought of her. Was she an irritation to him? Was he humouring her? Probably both. Yet, here she was, sitting in a police car on their way to visit someone who had questions to answer.

'What do you think?' asked Nolan. He sounded genuinely curious which was unusual for a man. Even more uncommon was the fact that he was probably going to listen also.

'I don't like coincidences,' said Bobbie.

'I'd noticed,' said Nolan, with a grin. Then he gestured with his head in the direction they were going. 'This is quite a gamble,' he added, almost as an afterthought.

It was. More for Nolan, though. The young detective had gone out on a limb now for her. If what they were doing turned out to be a fool's errand then it would rebound badly on him from both her father and Captain O'Riordan.

'Thanks,' she said, quietly.

Nolan shook his head dismissively. If he was feeling nervous about what they were doing then, to give him credit, he wasn't showing it. Nor was he hinting at blaming her if things should go wrong.

They passed the scene of the crime. Bobbie glanced down the street and at the house where her father was no doubt fending off questions from the Monk family and Fitzroy Belmont, although she knew he'd returned to his house to await news.

If only he knew.

The temptation to tell her father everything she suspected had been great, but it was effectively ruled out by O'Riordan. Instead, they fobbed the inspector off with some mouthwash about Bobbie's discoveries in connection with the two kidnappers. Bobbie had felt a stab of guilt about doing this, but what could she do? There were no good choices at this point.

How she would like to have chatted through her ideas about the case with him. Yet, he had made that impossible with his stance on her choice of career. A part of her realised that she was determined to prove him wrong. In doing so, it would break her heart, and probably his, too. She was all he had and he was afraid of losing her. No, there were no perfect choices. This was life, she supposed.

'Do you know much about Renat or Bugsy?' asked Bobbie. 'Are they the sort that might harm Violet?'

Nolan shrugged and said, 'I haven't come across them in my time. I don't know much about either of them. How about you, Tim?'

'I met Renat once. He's bigger than me. Not someone you would choose to tangle with.'

This made Nolan laugh. He quipped, 'You'd fight an elephant for a bet.'

Yeats grinned, and replied, 'I'm a changed man, Sean.'

Bobbie was stunned for a moment. She had only just realised that she did not know Nolan's name.

Sean.

She thought about it and decided it suited him, even though his looks were more Italian than Irish. Sean Nolan.

Nolan turned to Bobbie and glanced with his eyes towards Yeats, 'Tim's in love.'

'Good for you Detective Yeats,' said Bobbie before adding mischievously, 'I'm glad you have a civilising influence in your life. All men should have one.'

'You hear that, Sean? A civilising influence, she says.'

Bobbie and Nolan laughed at this; however, she wasn't sure if he was making a point to Nolan. A part of her hoped so.

Up ahead loomed the Metropolitan Museum of Art. There was a crowd outside as usual, milling around the steps. Bobbie could not understand why. The icy air would freeze the eyeballs of a penguin. Not a night to be out and about. They drove past the Met a couple of blocks. Then Nolan pointed to a sign that read E 86th Street.

'Turn here,' said Nolan.

Yeats turned onto the street and they drove a block before Nolan pointed to an apartment building with a blue awning extending from the double doors. Yeats pulled up outside. They stepped out of the car and hurried to the entrance. There was no doorman which was just as well as they would have been frozen solid standing outside.

The entrance comprised some faux marble steps that led up to elevators. There was a bank of buzzers to alert the apartment owners of visitors.

'We'll just go straight up,' said Nolan, heading up to the two elevators and pressing the call button. They waited in silence for the doors to open. Bobbie's heart was racing now as she genuinely had no idea what would happen next. They were here because of her. They would ask questions. But was this simply a wild goose chase like her intuition on the death of Hamilton Monk? A part of her refused to accept that this had been suicide. Something about the suicide note was nagging her. And she knew why it was nagging her. She hadn't shared this with Nolan yet.

She would soon, though.

A bell rang and the elevator doors opened. They stepped in and Nolan pressed the button for the third floor. No one was talking. Bobbie sneaked a glance at the two men with her. She could see some tension on their faces. There was no reason to believe they were in danger and yet, just then, she realised that this was not certain.

They could be walking into danger.

It shocked her to think that this was what it was like to be a detective. Every visit to question someone was a leap into the unknown. You could not be certain as to what awaited you on the other side of the door. She'd never thought of this before. Her own father had done this day after day, year after year and she had never thought of it. Not once. She couldn't breathe now. This was not because she was afraid, and she was, but because she felt shame. A deep shame at not having felt empathy for a man who not only had been a father to her, but also someone who had dedicated his life to making the world a safer place not just for her, but for everyone.

'Are you okay, Miss Flynn?' asked Nolan. He was studying her carefully. 'I think you should let us go first and you stay out of the way. We'll let you know when to come.'

Bobbie nodded, unable to speak lest it reveal her nervousness. For once she was not going to argue. She would only be in the way if there was any danger.

If.

It seemed so unlikely there would be, it was almost laughable, yet she now accepted that the two men with her could not assume that. Both men had their hands in their pockets and Bobbie suspected they were both clutching something reassuringly metallic.

The lift doors opened and they walked along the corridor, past two doors, until they arrived at their destination. Yeats checked the name plate. He nodded to Nolan. Bobbie stepped back to let them knock the door.

Nolan stood in front of the door while Yeats went to the wall. He nodded then Nolan knocked on the door.

No answer.

He knocked again. This time he heard noise from within the apartment. Someone said, 'Coming.'

The door opened and Nolan found himself staring at a small woman who was probably not a day younger than sixty. Nolan and the woman stared at one another for a moment then she spoke in a voice which had more than a hint of impatience in it.

'Well young man. What do you want?'

Nolan glanced behind the woman into a corridor with a door that was half open. He could see a Christmas tree.

'My name is Detective Nolan, from the New York Police Department. Are Mr and Mrs Belmont in?'

29

From somewhere deep inside Renat's slowly darkening world, a blackness that he wanted to give himself up to and lie back in its comforting embrace, he heard the screams of the little girl. His eyes shot open.

Above loomed a man, crouching down, fist held high in the air ready to deliver unto Renat the darkness he so badly wanted. Renat instantly regretted opening his eyes. He steeled himself for the blow. Then he passed out anyway.

The blow never came.

A bottle crashed against the man's head and he collapsed on top of Renat. The second man, who was standing crouched over the Russian, turned around to see what had happened to his pal. Afterwards, he reflected, this was his big mistake.

He caught the eye of the young girl. More importantly, the sight of her glaring angrily at him temporarily induced a form of paralysis that, upon reflection afterwards, he realised was calamitous. He noted dispassionately that she had withdrawn her arm, pitcher style. Seconds later he saw something flash through the air. With unerring accuracy, the bottle smacked him on the side of the head and he collapsed like a man on the gallows when the lever is pulled.

Screaming can only get you so far in life. Violet had learned this at an early age. It hadn't worked for her mother. It hadn't worked for her. The result was still the same. Pain. She'd watched Renat fall to the ground and one of the two men kneel down to begin raining blows upon the Russian. Now Lord knows there was probably no reason for Violet to feel anything towards a man who had been so instrumental in making this a pretty miserable day for her. She was cold, she was tired and she was hungry. Yet, somewhere within her ten, almost eleven-year-old mind a calculus had evolved whose conclusion was that she needed the Russian if she was to get home.

And he'd helped her when she was in difficulty. Fair's fair, she thought.

The bottles by the trash can were too obvious a gift to ignore. Without even thinking, she bent down and picked up a couple. She knew gin bottles when she saw them. They would do the job.

With an accuracy learned hurling stones on the streets of Hell's Kitchen, Violet fired off two missiles in the direction of her targets. Her aim would have made a marine sharpshooter nod in appreciation. For Violet, they were easy shots. The two men were barely fifteen yards away. Still, head shots were never easy and Violet always aimed for the head. Your quarry soon showed a little respect when they were ducking for their life.

Two bottles, two hits, two men unconscious. Not bad, she thought. She still had it. The sight of the two men collapsing to the ground, to add to the two that Renat had knocked out cold, warmed her greatly.

Up in one of the houses she saw some children looking out of the window. A boy of her age nodded and clapped in approval. Violet considered doing a curtsey, but then realised that she had to help Renat. At least she would have had it not been for the squeal of tyres behind her.

She spun around and saw that a car had drawn to a halt a few yards away. Certainly close enough for the young girl to remonstrate in a manner that made the driver's jaw fall open in shock.

'Are you Violet?'

Now it was Violet's turn to be rendered mute. She frowned and nodded. The driver turned to someone in the back of the car. Moments later the door swung open and a large man, almost the size of Renat, leapt out of the car. Without so much as a word of introduction, Violet was lifted into the air and deposited into the back of the car.

The door slammed shut. Violet looked up at the latest man to abduct her. The man looked back at her; consternation etched over his face. Violet glared back at him; eyes narrowed.

'Aren't you, Lenny Choynski?' she said, in a voice that was half angry, half shocked.

'Violet Scott?'

'Yes, who did you think I was?' responded Violet.

'We want Violet Belmont,' said Lenny.

'That's me,' replied Violet before noting the look of confusion on Lenny's face. 'I was fostered. You remember what a peach my dad was.'

'Yes, I remember. Your mom?'

'Dead.'

'I am sorry to hear that,' said Lenny and appeared to mean it.

I'm not thought Violet and felt a stab of guilt, at even having such a thought cross her mind. But why should she feel guilty? Her life had been miserable. Her mother had drunk herself to death and her father, well he was simply the most horrible man she would ever know. That's when he was around. Thankfully, it wasn't much.

Her life was so much better now. In fact, it began the day she'd met the Belmonts. They had chosen her, out of so many kids in the orphanage, to foster, even adopt. And she had been a model child. No parents could have had a more obedient and loving child. She had set out from the first day to make them want to adopt her.

And she was so close to that. She knew that they had submitted the papers. Why should it take so long she didn't know? A good lawyer is what you need, she'd joked. They all laughed.

Now she was in car with a man that she'd seen her father with many times. He wasn't a good man. Then again, the last time she'd seen him, he was threatening her father so perhaps there was some good in everyone.

'So, the Belmonts adopted you?'

'Fostered,' repeated Violet. Lenny nodded but was not too bothered about the distinction. She wasn't Eddie's kid any longer which was probably a good thing. That guy was one dumb mutt in Lenny's book. Not that Lenny read much.

Nature had bestowed upon Lenny a combination of size, below average looks and a predisposition towards violence. A career in the New York Police Department beckoned. Or crime. He chose the latter, reasoning that he could make more money while doing something that allowed high job satisfaction. A second cousin to the legendary fighter, Joe Choynski who had knocked out a young Jack Johnson, Lenny was built from similar fighting material. He was perfect henchman material and he loved his work. Mr Rothstein was a good employer and he considered himself a model employee.

'We're to bring you back,' said Lenny matter-of-factly. 'Those were Mr Rothstein's orders.'

Violet remembered her father had spoken of Mr Rothstein. His tone suggested that such a man was not to be crossed. So the news was probably good.

Violet began to shiver violently. The cold had now infiltrated her bones and she couldn't stop her teeth chattering. Lenny looked on in shock initially. Then he took off his overcoat and put it around the child.

'You are running around without a coat,' observed the father of three. Even henchmen have families.

Violet nodded, unable to speak. In truth, she wanted to cry, but it would not do in front of such a man. It wouldn't do, period. She turned her attention to the road. They were stuck in traffic so had barely moved from when they had picked her up.

'You're taking me home?'

'Looks like it, kid.'

Renat rolled the man off his body, before struggling to his feet. Around him lay four men. Three were conscious and groaning. One was on his hands and knees while the other two rolled around like they were having a nightmare. Violet's last victim was out for the count. There was glass sprinkled all around his bloodied head.

Renat's rise from the dead had coincided with seeing Violet carried into a car. The man who had done this looked familiar. Very familiar. What was his name? His brain was still somewhat scrambled by the beating he'd taken, although in part, Renat could not quite believe what he'd seen. His vision was a little blurred, head throbbed and he could feel blood on his forehead.

He knelt down and ransacked the pockets of the unconscious man. It produced two dollars. That would have to do. He grabbed his hat, then he staggered away from the scene of the carnage. Along the way, he passed an old man who quickly ducked into a doorway, to avoid the big Russian. A few people appeared at windows and a dog barked a goodbye. Renat didn't wave.

At the street corner he stuck a hopeful arm out at the passing traffic hoping a cab was passing. With his other arm, he cleaned his cheek of the blood. Snow was falling once more. He stuck his hand out to catch some of the flakes, before using it to clean his wound.

A cab appeared in the traffic. Renat held out the two dollars to incentivize the driver to stop for him. The driver saw the two dollars, sized up the Russian and decided to risk it. He stopped just in front of him. Renat climbed in and handed the driver the two dollars. He pointed to the Studebaker stopped up ahead.

'Follow grey car.'

30

Mrs Burley was not well-named. Standing four feet ten and weighing in at bantamweight, she had endured four decades of jokes about the mismatch between her name and her rather diminutive stature. She had loved her husband dearly, but not the name. Her husband, Stan, had laughed at every one of the jokes.

She missed him.

Her work as a housekeeper for the Belmonts was to see her into her pension, which was small. Just like her. She liked the job well enough without much liking the family. Of Violet she had not quite made up her mind. She was one part child of Satan, one-part evil witch. Between her and the child lay an uneasy truce. Mrs Belmont was a bit highly strung for Mrs Burley's tastes and the kidnapping of the hell child had only made this even more pronounced.

Mrs Burley's sympathies lay with the kidnappers. She could only begin to imagine the misery they were experiencing realising that, not only had they taken the wrong child, the child they had taken made it her life's work to be impossible.

She looked at the three people standing in the doorway. The first detective was a looker by any estimate. Forty years ago she might have thrown her hat into the ring. The policewoman with him was a doll. If they weren't breaking a bed by now, then she was clearly losing her marbles. She wasn't sure what to make of Yeats. Big, she supposed. She felt like a visitor from Lilliput alongside him.

'The Belmonts aren't in,' said Mrs Burley following Nolan's inquiry.

This was met with a frown.

'Where are they?'

'They went for a walk when Mr Belmont got back. They left twenty minutes ago.'

They were all standing at the door. Bobbie felt this was ridiculous. She smiled at the woman before them and said, 'Would you mind Mrs..?'

'Burley,' replied Mrs Burley.

Bobbie's face registered the look that the old woman had seen so often. She braced herself for a joke.

It never came.

'Mrs Burley, would you mind if we came in and waited for them?' asked Bobbie.

Mrs Burley was so grateful that a gilt-edged opportunity to repeat the joke she'd heard for nigh on forty years was to be passed up, she assented immediately.

They walked through to a very large living room that was decorated for Christmas. A large tree sat by the window, underneath which were presents. In the centre of the room were two brown leather Chesterfield sofas.

'Take a seat,' said Mrs Burley. 'Can I get you anything?'

They all shook their heads.

'It's a lovely apartment,' said Bobbie, with a smile. 'Could I take a look at Violet's room?'

'Of course,' replied Mrs Burley. 'Come this way.'

Neither Nolan nor Yeats were interested in this, so they sat down. It had occurred to Nolan that Bobbie seemed, without any effort, to have established a rapport with a woman that might otherwise have been suspicious and unhelpful. Once more, it occurred to him that the police would benefit greatly from giving more opportunities to women. In fact, it seemed all together remarkable that they had not made more than a few token appointments.

Bobbie followed Mrs Burley out of the room into a corridor with three doors. They went to the first door and Bobbie found herself inside Violet's bedroom. It was very tidy. There were some toys, but all had been neatly stacked into boxes. A small crucifix was on the wall over her bed. It was the bedroom of a young girl, no question.

'What is Violet like?' asked Bobbie.

Mrs Burley paused for a moment, which Bobbie noted, before saying, 'Spirited.'

'Spirited?' prompted Bobbie, one eyebrow raised.

'You know. Spirited.'

Bobbie probably did know but wanted to hear Mrs Burley say it. She, herself, could easily have been described in this way when she was ten or eleven. It went with the territory. Her father might have said a lot worse.

Mrs Burley paused to choose her words carefully, 'She came from the most awful circumstances. It's difficult to lose that.'

'In what way?' asked Bobbie.

'Well,' said Mrs Burley, fighting to find a path between stool-pigeon and disloyalty. 'She has a tongue on her. Not with the Belmonts, or even myself, but I do hear what she says and it's really not what one would expect from a young girl.'

'I see,' said Bobbie, stifling a grin. 'The room is very tidy, I must say. This is a credit to you, Mrs Burley.'

'Oh, nothing to do with me. She doesn't allow me in here,' said Mrs Burley, looking around the room as if it was her first time in it, also. 'She does keep it tidy; I'll say that.'

'How long have you been with the Belmonts?' asked Bobbie, changing the subject.

'Just over a year, year and a half. They took me on just before they took Violet in. I think they wanted help on parenting, more than tidying up and cooking.'

Just then, Nolan appeared at the door of the bedroom. Bobbie turned to him, with a question in her eyes.

'I think you should come back to the living room.'

The two ladies followed Nolan back down the corridor and into the living room where a surprise awaited them.

Violet Belmont was standing with Lenny Choynski. There was a certain mute tension in the air. It was clear that Yeats and Choynski knew one another and were unlikely to ever exchange cake recipes.

'Where's my mom and dad?' demanded Violet, to the adults in the room. She looked quite a sight. She had an overcoat draped over her shoulders that was seventeen sizes too large for her. It clearly belonged to Lenny.

'Lenny,' exclaimed Bobbie. 'You found her. I can't believe it.'

The heads of the two policemen spun around to Bobbie.

'You know this man?' cried Nolan in shock.

'I met him today,' explained Bobbie with a slightly embarrassed grin. 'He kindly agreed to help find Violet and he was true to his word. My word, Violet you look like you need a hot bath.'

Violet's eyes narrowed. For once she couldn't argue. She was tired, hungry and cold.

'Where's my mom and dad?' she asked once more. 'What are you doing here?'

Nolan and Yeats looked at Bobbie who, it seemed, was the one who was expected to answer. Bobbie went over to Violet and sat down so that her face was level with the young girl.

'I saw you earlier at the house,' said Violet, her eyes fixing on Bobbie.

'Yes, Violet,' replied Bobbie. 'I went to interview Mr Monk about his father. I work for a newspaper. These gentlemen are from the police. We came here to see how your mother and father were. I understand from Mrs Burley that they have gone out for a walk. It's been a trying day for them.'

'It was me that got kidnapped,' said Violet archly.

It was at that moment Bobbie decided she rather liked the young girl before her. Her eyes radiated more than just spirit and mischief, there was intelligence there too. She wasn't pretty, like Lydia Monk, but there was something compelling about her face. A sense of determination in the tilt of her head that almost, but not quite, hinted at arrogance.

Bobbie smiled at the child, 'You've been very brave. How did Lenny ever find you?'

'That's a long story,' said Violet.

Lenny took over at this point.

'I have a lot of friends and business associates,' said Lenny. 'I ask them to look for the young girl. When I ask, they do, if you know what I mean. I get a call an hour ago that a young girl is walking on the street with a big gentleman that I know to be Renat the Russian and my friends know this too. So we drive to look for said young girl and Renat the Russian, who is in serious trouble with many people.'

'He saved my life,' interrupted Violet.

'So you have told me Violet,' continued Lenny, 'But he does a very bad thing when he kidnaps you so we must make an example of him when we find him.'

Nolan wasn't having this, 'You will hand him over to the police Choynski if you find him, or me and Yeats here will make your life a misery.'

Lenny gave a half-smile at this before replying, 'Of course, Detective Nolan. Me and my associates believe in the rule of law and order. Now, I think it is time that we are leaving you.' With that he doffed his hat to Bobbie, nodded to Mrs Burley and scowled at the two policemen.

Then, with a surprising degree of gentleness, he took the large overcoat from the shoulders of Violet. Underneath the coat, Bobbie was shocked at how bedraggled the young girl was and it was clear she was shivering. Bobbie turned to Mrs Burley, but the housekeeper was already on the move. She took Violet's hand and led her towards the corridor. Violet did not object. She stopped at the door.

'Thanks Lenny,' she said. 'I mean it, Lenny. Don't hurt Renat.' With that said, she disappeared off with Mrs Burley.

This comment was met with a momentary silence and then Lenny said, 'We do not know where Renat is. Violet says he saved her life. Some men tried to grab her.'

'Other men, you mean. Where was this?' asked Nolan.

'Harlem.'

'Were they holding Violet in Harlem?' asked Nolan.

'No,' said Lenny. 'She tells me that she leaves their company through an open window and runs away. But Renat finds her. Then he says that he is taking her back to the museum. He says the person who hires them to swipe the Monk kid, tells them to leave Violet at the Met on 5th. I am guessing that the said person tells the Belmonts this also.'

Nolan turned to Yeats and said, 'I'll bet you that's where the Belmonts have gone. They think Violet is going to be dropped off at the Met.'

'On my way,' said Yeats.

The big policeman went to the front door. Lenny fixed his eyes on Nolan, 'You want anything more from me detective?'

Aside from putting you in jail, thought Nolan, no. Nolan shook his head. Lenny nodded to him and followed Yeats out the door.

As the front door shut, Nolan turned to Bobbie and asked the question uppermost in his mind.

'What do you make of all this?'

31

A combination of bad luck and bad weather meant that within a matter of minutes, Renat's cab had lost their quarry. This was frustrating on a number of levels. He felt a surprising degree of responsibility towards the child. She had proved to be unusually spirited for someone from these shores. He respected that. More worryingly, he could not be sure if the latest people to abduct the child had criminal intentions. The irony of this consideration was lost on the big Russian.

'I lost 'em, bud,' said the cab driver, turning to Renat. As he was in possession of the two dollars, he was profoundly unworried by the development. 'What do you want me to do?'

Renat thought about this. Mother Nature had not bestowed him with a reflective mind. It had compensated him, instead, with fists that could separate most men from their senses. Right at that moment he would have traded it all to have a decent plan on what to do. He soon realised there was only one thing he could.

'Met.'

'Met?'

'Met,' replied Renat.

'Opera or Art?' asked the Cab driver.

There was more than one? Had these people so little imagination that they named everything cultural the same?

'Art,' said Renat, hoping to hell that he had understood Bugsy correctly. Just then, he wondered, for the first time, where his comrade in arms was. Perhaps Bugsy had made it to the Met also.

The last time Bugsy had visited an art gallery was when he had helped steal a painting, on behalf of a business associate who had a taste for Cubist art. His taste was not shared by Bugsy who thought the painting ridiculous and the price tag attached to it even more so. Who did this Picasso think he was anyway? Bugsy's niece in Philly could paint better and she was only in second grade.

As Renat was careering along an icy road to the Metropolitan Museum of Art, Bugsy was bitterly regretting his decision to drive to Philadelphia. The roads were treacherous and that was only with the number of police cars he had seen. The snow was, quite literally, the icing on this particular cake. On the plus side, every mile away from New York was a good thing, but the snowflakes assaulting his windscreen were the size of baseballs and it was a long time since Bugsy had felt such overwhelming unease. But he was committed now.

All thoughts of Renat, and that hellish child, were out the window. She'd find a cop and then all would be good. He just hoped that Renat would read the runes and get the hell out of town. The last thing he needed was the big lug to be caught by the police and to turn stool-pigeon on him. The thought of this sent an involuntary shiver through his body and he was already pretty cold to begin with.

Traffic slowed down on the road he was on. Bugsy wasn't sure if this was a desire to drive more carefully or if there had been an accident. He'd already passed three on the journey so far.

Then he saw the cause. There was a police check point. Bugsy's heart went into his mouth. If there is a more vulnerable feeling than talking to the police while you are in a stolen car, then Bugsy was damned if he knew it.

The next half hour was torture as the car snaked its way, slowly, up to its meeting with nemesis. There was no way Bugsy could turn away as it would arouse suspicion. No, he had to hope that a combination of weather and night time would be his friend.

Soon Bugsy was winding his window down and addressing an old cop, who no more wanted to be out on a night like this than he did.

'Awful night officer,' said Bugsy, sketching a weak smile.

'Sure is,' agreed the policeman.

'So, what's up anyway?' asked Bugsy, showing the policeman his driver's licence.

'You heard about the kidnapping of that kid?' asked the policeman while giving the licence a quick scan and then looking at the back of the car.

'Yeah awful,' agreed Bugsy.

'Yeah, awful. I don't know what kind of low scum bags, would do such a thing,' said the policeman. Bugsy bridled at being described thus, but rejected the idea of defending the kidnappers with a point about everyone has to make a living and he was sure they would treat the child well. The policeman handed back the licence and said, 'I hope they catch these guys and put 'em in prison for life. The inmates will deal with them all right.'

Bugsy gulped and smiled once more, He nodded to the policeman and was soon on his way. And, for the next two hours, he could think of nothing else but the prospect of being beaten to a pulp by the righteously indignant, justice-seeking inmates of Sing Sing.

The prospect of Sing Sing was looming large in Renat's mind too. Having grown up in the dark, icy tundra of northern Russia, Renat was not one to shy away from the hard reality of life. He didn't believe in luck any more than he was convinced there was a divine spirit guiding humankind towards a virtuous life. Paradoxically, he believed in evil. He had seen it first-hand, escaped from it in Russia, only to find it had a different skin in America and you could vote for them every four years. And he was in the tightest spot he had faced since his escape from the Red Army. This tight spot took the form of a moral dilemma and a practical problem.

He could do what he had done in Russia and fly. America was a big place. It would be easy to get lost, even for someone like him. He was big. There was always a market somewhere for someone like him.

Yet, he knew he could not do this. He had to make sure that the child was returned. Safely. Why this should be so, he could not fathom. As misadventures went, this would be one to tell the grandchildren about if he ever had any. Kidnapping, then losing the kidnap victim not once, but twice. By any standard, that took some doing.

Now he was heading into the teeth of a potential storm without the aid of any map to guide him. He did not know what Violet's parents looked like. He didn't know where she lived, but perhaps he could find out.

He did know the man who had taken Violet. That was another solution, but not one he sought. Lenny Choynski was a not a man to be on the wrong side of and, certainly, not his boss, Arnold Rothstein.

'That's the Met up there,' said the cab driver, pointing to the enormous façade of the museum that might have been described as neoclassical, but certainly not by the former Russian peasant. It was lit in an orange glow against the ink-black sky. Renat's heart sank, as he saw hundreds of people milling around on the steps. It's difficult to find someone in such a crowd. It's even more difficult if you don't know what they look like.

The cab drew to a halt outside the museum, causing several people to come over thinking that the cab would be available. When they reached the cab, they took one look at Renat's face and decided against inquiring if it was free.

'Hey, look at that,' said the cabbie.

Renat was looking. He saw a police car pull up in front of them and a policeman leap out onto the sidewalk. He seemed to be looking for someone also, if the jerking of his head left and right was any sign. They observed the detective walking around in frustration. There was no question he was looking for someone and Renat's guess was he was looking for Violet and her parents.

Who clearly were not there.

Renat stared out at the scene, feeling a combination of guilt and confusion. Perhaps there were better ways to earn a living than what he had done. Threatening debtors or being a bodyguard for gang leaders seemed a wholly innocent career by comparison.

Then an idea struck him that seemed so extraordinary he could barely believe that he had thought of it. Unquestionably, it was a risk. Nevertheless, its audacity was perhaps what gave it the remarkably slim chance of succeeding. Because for all of the trip up 5th Avenue, Renat's mind had been forced to cogitate on the situation that had brought him here. And one notion had taken root that he could not shake. The gamble he was about to undertake would put this suspicion to the ultimate test, Renat's freedom.

'I go,' said Renat to the cab driver.

The cabbie could care less. A fare that was probably less than a dollar had earned him two.

'Happy new year,' said the delighted cabbie as the door closed.

Renat rarely felt any apprehension. When you are six feet six and built like an ocean liner, you are pretty well equipped to deal with most of life's exigencies, although this may require a certain moral laxity from time to time.

He strode forward, with more purpose than he was feeling, towards the detective who appeared to be built on a similar scale to himself. Then he stopped. Perhaps it was last minute stage fright. Was this an act of madness? Unquestionably. He didn't need to be here. He could be on a box car heading out of the city right now. As doubts assailed him his chance to run came and went.

Detective Yeats turned around and saw a man he knew to be Renat the Russian standing a few feet away from him.

If Renat's head was a swirling vortex of uncertainty, Yeats' head was anything but. Within seconds he had a gun in his hand and it was pointing it at the big Russian's chest. Yeats was not a man to feel trepidation in the face of physical risk, but even he thought the gun looked rather small, when set against the Russian's bulk.

Renat put his hands up and stepped forward. There was a frown on his face.

'I look for girl,' said Renat to the bemused detective.

32

A few minutes after the departure of Yeats to find the Belmont couple, Bobbie and Nolan heard the sound of a key in the front door. They were alone in the front room as Mrs Burley had gone to attend to Violet, running a bath and helping her get changed.

'That was quick,' said Nolan in surprise as the door swung open, expecting to see his colleague. It was not him. Instead, the Belmonts walked into the apartment. There was no sign of Yeats.

'Who the hell...' began Fitzroy Belmont, until he recognised the detective and then Bobbie as the young woman he'd seen earlier.

Olivia Belmont walked in and looked shaken. The last day must have been horrible for her, thought Bobbie. Olivia frowned for a moment as she tried to place the young woman who was standing uninvited in her apartment.

'What's going on? What's happened to Violet?' exclaimed Olivia, her voice tinged by hysteria. 'Has something happened?'

'She's home safe and sound,' said Nolan, who was on his feet now. His voice was reassuring and immediately appeared to calm the couple down.

Olivia looked around her and saw no sign of Violet.

'She's in the bath. Mrs Burley is with her,' explained Bobbie.

The couple immediately ran from the room to check on this. Moments later, Bobbie and Nolan heard the shouts of joy coming from the bathroom down the corridor.

'We may as well sit down,' said Nolan.

They stayed there in silence for a few minutes, while the reunion of the family took place. Then Fitzroy Belmont appeared and walked over to his cocktail cabinet. He was about to treat himself to a drink, when he realised that he had a policeman in his house. He stopped and turned.

'Go ahead,' said Nolan with a half-smile. 'Don't mind me. Stupid law in my book.'

'Thanks,' said Belmont. He picked up the cocktail shaker and then held it in the direction of Nolan.

The detective shook his head as did Bobbie when he gestured to her.

'I definitely need one,' said the lawyer. 'It's been quite a day; I can tell you.'

It took another minute and then he poured himself a cocktail from the silver shaker. Then he walked over to the sofa and sat down opposite Bobbie and Nolan. Bobbie had shifted her seat and joined Nolan when Belmont arrived.

'My wife will join us in a minute,' said Belmont.

'I understand,' replied Nolan. 'Take your time. I'm sure this has been a trying day.'

'You have no idea,' agreed Belmont. 'What on earth happened?'

'When your wife comes, we'll update you. It appears young Violet proved quite a handful for the kidnappers,' said Nolan.

You're telling me, thought Belmont.

Another minute passed in an awkward silence, until Belmont, tired of waiting, called down the corridor for his wife to join them. He wanted the visitors out as soon as possible.

Of course, since the dawn of time, no wife worthy of the name has responded immediately to the reasonable request of a husband to hasten to her beloved. Thus, another minute passed before an evidently irritated Olivia Belmont appeared, glaring at her husband, because, obviously, he was to blame for the continued presence of the visitors.

'Yes?' she snapped in the general direction of the cocktail cabinet.

'Mrs Belmont,' began Nolan. 'We thought you would like to hear more about what we understand to have caused the return of your daughter.'

Nolan paused for a moment and took the lady's angry silence as permission to continue.

'As I was telling your husband, it seems your...Violet, that is, escaped from the abductors who we know to be two men, a Bugsy McDaid and Renat Murdrych. This remarkable young lady, then made her escape by walking alone, for quite some time, before she was apprehended again by Renat the Russian. Now, this is where things become a little confused. Apparently, she is alleging that Renat actually saved her life at this point, as she was under threat from some men that she had encountered during her escape and that he was, in fact, intending to take her back.'

'Really,' exclaimed Belmont, turning to his wife 'That's extraordinary. I almost find it impossible to believe. I suspect she is still in shock. Confused. I might add, if you don't mind me saying, that she really shouldn't have been questioned without her parents...'

'Or a lawyer?' suggested Nolan with a straight face.

'No, indeed, without a lawyer present.'

'As it happens, the story is not quite complete. It seems that Renat was good to his word because they made their way over 3rd Avenue Bridge and were in Harlem when they were attacked by another group of four men. Violet, once more, alleges that Renat the Russian saved her life by fighting them off while she escaped.'

'I find that extraordinary,' interjected Belmont. 'You know Violet has quite an imagination.'

'This would certainly be something we would consider were it not for the fact that Violet was, at this point, picked up by a second man, a man who is very well known to the police in the city for reasons that have nothing to do with his good nature. This man, under orders from a man that we would very much like to see incarcerated, was instructed to find Violet and return her to her own home. He received a tip off from a community-minded individual that people answering the description of Violet and Renat the Russian had been seen walking through Harlem together.'

'I could scarcely believe this if I read it in a book,' suggested Belmont.

'I imagine the readers would be struggling to suspend disbelief by this point also, but this is exactly what occurred. They found Violet in the middle of heated battle between Renat and the attackers. Violet, apparently took out two of the men by throwing glass bottles.'

'She's the star pitcher in her baseball team,' said Belmont edgily.

'Not softball?' asked Bobbie, genuinely surprised Violet was not playing the gentler, more junior, version of America's game.

Belmont shook his head resignedly, 'No, she found it a bit tame. Before she came to the house, it seems she developed a remarkable facility for throwing things with a high degree of precision.'

'Lenny Choynski would certainly testify to that,' replied Nolan. 'I gather she laid out two hoodlums with, as you say, a high degree of precision. You should let the Yankees know, Mr Belmont. It was Lenny Choynski who returned Violet just before you returned from your walk.'

Olivia Belmont burst into tears and was immediately comforted by her husband.

'Where did you go, Mr Belmont? I suspect you just missed Mr Choynski,' asked Nolan.

'We went for a walk around the block. We needed to clear our heads,' said Belmont.

'Not towards the Met, then?' asked Bobbie, in as innocent a manner as is possible from a redhead.

'No,' said Belmont. 'Why do you ask?'

'Apparently that was the agreed drop off point for the child. Not your house. Are you saying that the kidnappers were not in contact with you to arrange such a drop off?'

'No,' snapped Belmont indignantly. 'What are you saying?'

What Nolan would like to have said is "I think you are lying". There were a number of reasons why the lawyer might lie, chief among which was to see an end to the affair and ensure that there was no reoccurrence. This would make complete sense and Nolan understood his reluctance to admit that the kidnappers had been in contact.

Any further conversation was interrupted by a knock on the door.

'Who the hell..?' appeared to be a favourite saying of Belmont or would have been had he actually said "hell" rather than something that immediately required a public recantation as two ladies' heads snapped in his direction. Rather than suffer longer in the looks of reproach from his wife and female visitor and, it must be said, Bobbie's was laid on a little thick as she, herself, was not beyond the occasional profanity in moments of strain, Belmont leapt to his feet and went to the door.

The door opened and he found himself facing a very tall, very large, foreign-looking man. He stumbled into the apartment followed by yet another large man holding a gun.

For the third time, in as many minutes, Belmont uttered his catchphrase which was unlikely to find its way into the Ziegfeld Follies any time soon.

Nolan and Bobbie were surprised to see the new arrivals. As this was New York and relatively high society, Nolan decided that introductions were probably in order.

'This is Detective Yeats, Mr Belmont. And this, unless I miss my guess, is one of the kidnappers, Renat Murdrych, the kidnapper of your daughter.'

33

While Nolan may not have been surprised by the arrival of Detective Yeats, the capture of Renat was an unexpected bonus. More than this, it was quite a coup and begged so many questions his mind was a whirl as he considered them.

Bobbie was also in a state of shock. The size of the Russian was quite something to behold. He made even Lenny Choynski seem like a pygmy by comparison. Renat's hat was soaked a much darker shade of grey and his overcoat had threadbare patches which would be no defence against the cold and the wet snow. The sound of his breathing was like a bear snoring. He cut a disconsolate figure and it made Bobbie wonder why he was here.

The shock was momentary, but it was long enough to allow Fitzroy Belmont to spring towards the giant, whose arms were hanging limply in front of him, his hands in handcuffs and smacked him across the face before Nolan, seeing what was about to happen, hopped to his feet and restrained the angry lawyer. Renat barely batted an eyelid. The punch had all the destructive effect of a fly landing on an elephant's tusk.

Belmont continued to struggle after a fashion. The job of restraining the lawyer was not as challenging as one might have supposed for a man of his size. He was of medium height, but quite powerfully built. However, Belmont was but a middleweight compared to the heavyweight Russian. Nolan would still have bet on Renat even with two arms quite literally tied behind his back. The detective, while slender, had a rangy build that was more powerful than it looked, and he had no trouble manhandling the lawyer back to the sofa.

'You dirty…' said Belmont and added a few more words that Bobbie decided to let go because she would have said similar, or worse, in Belmont's shoes.

'Isn't this nice,' said Nolan, recovering his shock at the turn of events. 'Good work Tim. Where on earth did you find him?'

'He was at the Met. He said he was looking for the kid, sorry, for Violet.'

Belmont made another attempt at grabbing the Russian. It wasn't much of an effort and even Olivia Belmont seemed faintly irritated by his transparent desire to be held back.

'He should be in jail. Why have you brought him here?' demanded Belmont. 'Do you want him to go and kidnap my daughter again?' screamed Belmont. Then his face twisted into a smile as he said, 'You're a vile beast. You know what they do to people like you in prison?'

Everyone looked at Renat and thought that not very much would happen to him unless the attacker had a strong desire to visit the hospital or the mortuary.

Nolan fixed his eyes on the Russian. This required him to look up which is something he rarely had to do with another man as he was slightly above six feet himself. Nolan glanced down at the handcuffs. They could barely fit the big man's wrists. He shot Yeats a glance and said, 'I'm amazed you caught him.'

'He came quietly,' admitted Yeats. 'He just put his hands out and I cuffed him. He said he just wanted to find the girl.'

'Is this true?' snapped Nolan, turning to Renat.

'I look for girl,' said the garrulous gangster. His face betrayed no emotion. He'd done with emotions four years ago. All except a couple. The anger remained. So did the hatred.

'Why?' asked Nolan. He asked it in a cop's way, pressing forward. Demanding. Yet there was just a note of perplexity in his voice too, which Bobbie picked up on. She understood why it would be there.

'Why?'

The question brought a moment's silence from Renat. Bobbie could have sworn that he was embarrassed. He certainly seemed sheepish. His gaze shot to the floor and his voice was a low rumble of guilt, bubbling like the surface of a geyser.

'I lost her,' admitted Renat.

'How?' pressed Nolan.

This brought another elongated pause before the Russian answered, 'We were attacked. Lenny Choynski took her.'

'Did Lenny attack you?' prompted Nolan.

'No.'

Nolan nodded. So far, so true.

'Why were you bringing her back?' asked Bobbie, stepping forward, but staying within arm's reach of cover, in this case the handsome figure of Detective Nolan. This brought a half-smile from the detective as the rationale behind Bobbie's choice of positioning was all too obvious.

'Wrong girl.'

'So what did you want to do?' asked Bobbie, feeling a little bit more confident now and stepping away from Nolan. It had occurred to her, also, that she may get more from the Russian if she wasn't peeking over Nolan's shoulder calling out questions. If the little girl Violet had faced this man down, then so could she.

'Told to bring girl back.'

'Who told you?' asked Nolan. He moved closer to the Russian, his eyes never left Renat's.

'The boss.'

'Who is your boss? What is his name - the man that hired you?' asked Nolan. Renat seemed nonplussed by this. It was as if he did not understand the question. Nolan tried again only more slowly, 'Did you understand my question? Who hired you.'

'I don't know,' said Renat with a shrug. 'Maybe Bugsy know.'

'Where is Bugsy?' asked Nolan.

'I don't know.'

'So you don't know who the man that hired you is? Bugsy never said a name?' asked Nolan.

Renat shook his head. He shifted his gaze towards Bobbie. This made Bobbie's blood freeze momentarily yet, almost immediately, she relaxed. There was something that was oddly unthreatening about Renat despite his size. If she had to describe what she saw in the Russian, it was a sense of regret.

His next statement was like a thunderclap during a monk's meditation.

'Not a man. A woman.'

This revelation was only slightly less shocking than the next thing that was said. Bobbie wheeled around from the Russian.

She was in the middle of the room, between Nolan on one side, Renat and Yeats on another and the Belmonts, both sitting on the Chesterfield. Not a man, a woman the Russian had said.

'And that woman was you, Mrs Belmont. Wasn't it?' said Bobbie, pointing to Olivia Belmont.

34

It took a few seconds for the accusation to land onto the collective mind of the room and then all hell broke loose. It was like the starter's pistol in a race, the first cannon being fired in a battle, the first nervous call of a general swirling his sword in the air shouting to a thousand reluctant soldiers, "follow me men".

Fitzroy Belmont was on his feet in a moment. His face had turned red, there was a very real danger that an eyeball pop out and be projected across the room. He was pretty miffed in any Englishman's book, if anyone from that island race had been present.

'How dare you,' screamed Belmont causing Bobbie to duck some recalcitrant flecks of spittle. Belmont was aware that his rage was somewhat undermined by the errant saliva and Olivia Belmont buried her head in her hands, as much from embarrassment as a desire to convey distress at an unjust and unfounded accusation.

Belmont edged forward as if he was going to attack Bobbie, but Nolan by the merest shift of his stance, effectively discouraged such an idea.

'Are you just going to stand there and allow this, this, this...'

'Woman?' offered Nolan.

'This mad woman to hurl unwarranted accusations in the direction of someone who has suffered unimaginably because of this, this, this...'

'Hoodlum,' suggested Nolan, glancing in the direction of Renat. The Russian was impassive about much of what was happening. This was, of course, his usual demeanour so it was nothing unusual, but his mind was very much spinning with what the young woman had said. It is not a henchman's lot to be a great thinker. When Rodin sculpted his masterpiece, it is unlikely he had a six-foot six henchman in mind as he wondered how a great thinker might emerge from the lump of clay he had in his hands. Renat had a lot to think about.

And this would take time.

Bobbie, having survived the initial verbal onslaught, which your chronicler has left unreported, due to the robust nature of the language, stepped forward.

'It was never your intention to kidnap Violet. What would be the point? No, Lydia Monk was the target. As we know a mistake was made and your best laid plans went badly awry.'

This was met with yet another fusillade from Fitzroy, but he was shushed by Renat who was all ears about what had happened. When you are shushed by a six foot six Russian, it is best to refrain from further comment. Belmont wisely said nothing but did send a scowl in the direction of Renat, which he hoped would convey that he was far from finished with the kidnapper.

Bobbie was now fully committed to her course and she was gratified to see that Nolan was prepared to let her hold court. Yeats, who was somewhat late to the investigation said nothing as he had no idea what was going on, but a great view of the attractive accuser and this suited him fine.

'And these plans have been a year in the making, haven't they?'

This comment stunned Olivia Belmont out of her self-imposed suffering. Her head shot up, eyes widened in shock, as if the speaker had just emphasized a point by breaking wind. Nolan kept his eyes on the Belmonts, but he would love to have looked at the inspector's daughter at that moment for a whole host of reasons that did not bear thinking about.

'Yes, it was over a year in the planning,' repeated Bobbie. Her voice was strong and certainty cascaded through every syllable. 'Your firm has been losing customers for some time. You needed money. Changing the will was one way of course. You engineered a meeting with Hamilton Monk to update the existing will. Then you changed it didn't you? You used Freddy the Forger to do this. He forged the signature of Hamilton Monk on the new will, a will in which you awarded yourselves ten thousand dollars.'

Olivia Belmont's mouth fell open and not in a good way. Her husband dismissed this accusation with another volley of abuse.

'I saw the will,' interrupted Bobbie. 'I'm sure that a handwriting expert will be able to confirm that you had the signature forged. It's why you had to kill Freddy. You couldn't afford to have him running loose, especially when you successfully accomplished the second part of your plan. So you murdered him and then you faked the suicide of Hamilton Monk.'

'This is absurd,' bellowed Belmont. 'If you don't stop her, I shall.' He pointed to Nolan, before getting once more to his feet. He was quickly disabused of progressing with this initiative by the sight of both Renat and Nolan closing ranks around Bobbie. He sat down again in something of a huff.

'You killed Hamilton Monk in the garden summerhouse and you casually left a suicide note provided by, the now deceased, Freddy. The killer escaped through the bathroom window at the back knowing that it would take Froome and the kitchen staff at least a minute to make it to the summerhouse.'

'And then, I sprouted wings and flew away from the scene of the crime,' sneered the lawyer.

'No, you simply hid behind the house and then escaped when you had the chance to go back in through the French windows of the dining room.' Bobbie sneaked a glance at Olivia Belmont. She had turned very pale in the face of the accusations. This was not a sign of guilt, but Bobbie knew what she was saying was hitting home.

'Two murders and all to get ten thousand dollars. And still it was not enough. In fact, it was never meant to be. This was simply a smokescreen for the bigger plan. The plan to kidnap Lydia Monk. A plan that was born over a year ago, when you fostered a ten-year-old girl, with the express idea of having her befriend Lydia and, unwittingly, lure her into the trap.'

Nolan could scarcely believe what he was hearing, yet he knew instinctively that the man he was staring at, the couple even, had indeed done just what Bobbie had said. It was written all over their faces, their postures, the fake anger of their reactions.

Their reactions did not ring true for the simple reason that they were faked. And Nolan knew that Bobbie was waiting to play her ace. It was an ace that she could play because they had a piece of evidence that was, quite literally, enormous.

They had the kidnapper. They had Renat.

That the kidnapper would not be able to identify the people that hired him was unimportant as Bobbie, Nolan realised, was waiting to point out.

'Do you have even a single piece of evidence, to support these ludicrous claims? You do know that this is real life, don't you? It isn't some dime novel, where the gifted amateur detective lays out the charges and the idiot villain confesses all immediately,' snarled Belmont, before adding his final point to dismiss Bobbie. 'Where is your evidence?'

As he said this, Belmont was glancing nervously at Renat. There were many reasons why one would glance nervously at such a man mountain and Bobbie suspected he was thinking the same as she was at that moment. She would enjoy this.

'We know that your firm has been suffering. It's why you made Marcus Fisher your partner. It's where you were able to meet Freddy, the Forger and contact Bugsy McDaid and Renat. It's no coincidence that Mr Fisher represents all of these men as clients.'

'Hardly evidence,' pointed out Belmont, with a contemptuous wave of his hand.

'True,' admitted Bobbie, seemingly defeated. A smile crossed the face of Belmont similar to one you would see on a jackal as a bunch of lions depart a carcass looking for somewhere to grab forty winks. Then she straightened up, 'But, perhaps, the house you rented in the Bronx might count. You are the same Mr Fitzroy Belmont, who rented a small house with, unusually, a telephone?'

This was unexpected. Belmont's eyes widened and he looked from Bobbie and then to the Russian. Beads of perspiration broke out on his forehead. He stared at Renat, the one man who could link him and his wife to that house.

'I'm a little new to this game,' interjected Nolan, 'but I think that does sound like evidence to me, wouldn't you say Mr Belmont?' A smile crossed his face as he stared at the lawyer who seemed broken by this news. Then the smile left Nolan's face as he stared down the barrel of a 9-millimetre Astra 400.

35

One hour earlier – Midtown precinct

Captain Francis O'Riordan had a decision to make. In fact, he had a number. The news that the young woman, who he had taken a huge dislike to had, apparently, struck gold again with, yet another, lucky guess. He didn't want to contemplate the unthinkable, that she was actually rather good at this. Should he acknowledge her contribution and, more importantly, should he go to the site that they thought might be the location of the kidnapped child or should he go to the apartment of the lawyer and be in on the capture of the mastermind of the crime.

This was not a difficult choice on either count. Headlines were made when children were involved. This could launch him towards becoming Chief of Police. City Hall, maybe. His eyes hardened.

'Thanks Fleischer,' said O'Riordan before adding in a low voice, directed towards an empty desk. 'Good work. Right, we have to move quickly. Yeats, tell uniform to get to the address Fleischer just said. Fleischer, you, me and Harry will go there. Nolan and Yeats get down to the Belmonts' apartment.'

'Uniform?' asked Nolan.

'No, not yet. I'll send some patrolmen if we find the kid. At this point, I just want you there to question them, but don't tip your hand. Make up some moonshine that the kidnappers called again and they will call the Belmonts' apartment. Think of something.'

The only thing Nolan was thinking was the same as what everyone else in the office was, O'Riordan, who had done nothing so far in the investigation, wanted to steal himself the glory.'

'Yes sir,' said Nolan.

Minutes later, O'Riordan was in a car being driven by Fleischer and speeding up towards the Bronx. The journey took twenty minutes as they encountered traffic snarled up by the weather. They arrived at the street that Fleischer had found.

'Pull over here, out of sight,' said O'Riordan to Fleischer, who had already mostly done this. Fleischer caught the smile on Harrigan's face when he turned around and the roll of the eyes.

The three men jumped out of the car and walked towards the house.

'Fleischer, see if there is an alleyway around the back. Harry, you come with me. We'll go through the front. Where the hell are those patrolmen? I hope they don't come tearing along with their sirens blowing, waking up the dead.'

Fleischer peeled away from his two colleagues and disappeared down one street while O'Riordan and Harrigan slowly made their way towards the house. It was a strange street. There were tenements on either side of the street and a few houses, as well as a corner store. The street was virtually empty except for a few old, rather battered cars parked by the sidewalk.

A cold wind stung the faces of the two men as they reached the house. O'Riordan pointed to Harrigan to keep walking past the house to see if there was any sign of life inside. By now, O'Riordan's senses were tingling and the message they were sending his brain were consistent and not good.

They were too late.

At the same moment, the two men darted towards the front door. They pulled out their Colts and then Harrigan rapped the door with his fist.

'Bugsy, Renat, it's the police. You're surrounded.' Just then, rather serendipitously, a police siren wailed nearby and then another. The troops were arriving. 'Do you hear me. Open up or it'll be the worse for you, Bugsy.'

O'Riordan now had a bad feeling about this. Time to act. He nodded to Harrigan, so they stood back from the door and at the same moment kicked it open. They charged into the house that was as cold as it was utterly empty. The silence was broken by the sound of O'Riordan screaming obscenities to an uncaring world.

It was as O'Riordan was giving vent to his frustration that the patrolmen arrived on the scene and quite a scene it was. O'Riordan was now bent double with anger. Harrigan, looking on in an amused manner, was lighting up a cigar that had been stolen from the Chief of Police with whom he shared a taste in expensive tobacco.

Patrolmen flooded into the room. One old grizzled old cop looked around and then fixed a look on Harrigan.

'Has the bird flown the coop,' asked the police sergeant, whose name was Elroy.

'Looks like it,' nodded Harrigan.

Just then an elderly man pushed his way through the crowd of patrolmen and asked, 'Who is in charge here?'

In a response that would, coincidentally, have found favour with the man that Bobbie and Nolan were visiting, O'Riordan straightened up and asked something not very along the lines of, 'And who the hell are you?'

The rather cranky response, from the detective, temporarily silenced the old man and then he smiled sympathetically and replied, 'If you are looking for those men and that young girl, they left an hour or two ago.'

O'Riordan could scarcely believe what he was hearing.

'Left?' he repeated as if he hadn't quite heard correctly.

''Yes, left,' confirmed the old man, now fully convinced he was dealing with an idiot.

O'Riordan walked forward towards the man in a manner that would have been threatening in a speakeasy, or a saloon in 1877, but seemed ridiculous in this context.

'Why didn't you call the police?'

Now there were several answers to this question and the man, faced with such a paradox of choice, shook his head, and shrugged. O'Riordan, rather like the old man, was certain he, too, was facing an idiot.

'You do realise these men were kidnappers. And the young girl had been abducted.'

'Well, sir,' began the man, 'it seems the young girl un-abducted herself if what I saw is what I saw.'

O'Riordan looked askance at the man. He shook his head and turned to the men and asked, 'Can someone tell me what this man is saying?'

Harrigan had an inkling and said, 'Hey bud, are you saying the young girl escaped.'

'That's exactly what I'm saying.'

'Gee, I wish you'd told us,' said O'Riordan with heavy sarcasm and gesturing to the assembled, and rather large, crowd of police now in the front room and outside.

'Well sir,' replied the old man with equally heavy sarcasm. 'I didn't know she'd been kidnapped. And even if I did, I don't have a phone.'

'Payphone?' suggested Harrigan, thoroughly amused by the old man's defiance. He took a drag on his cigar and waited for the response.

'Some kids robbed it. Doesn't work,' said the old man.

'Well ain't that just dandy,' replied a thoroughly unhappy police captain.

At this point, Fleischer appeared from a back room. He walked into the front room and, before taking in the fact that there was a large crowd of policemen, he said, 'Hey Cap, there's no one back here.'

All eyes fell on Fleischer, including two full of molten fury from his captain.

Twenty minutes later, O'Riordan, Harrigan and Fleischer were pulling up outside the apartment building, where the Belmonts lived. They passed the police car that clearly had carried Nolan and Yeats to the apartments earlier. This, at least, was good news. It meant they were still there. O'Riordan was already planning how he could make a virtue of necessity and be in on the bust of the lawyer. It was frustrating that he could not bring the child in. It was equally frustrating that, even if he did make the bust, everyone in the precinct would be giving credit to that interfering daughter of Inspector Flynn.

'Let's go,' said O'Riordan. Once more Harrigan and Fleischer exchanged looks. The captain was one of those leaders who insisted on ordering people to do something they were either already doing or were intending to do anyway.

The two men were out of the car and jogging after O'Riordan. The captain was, quite literally, a man on a mission. The elevator doors opened just as they reached them.

It was empty.

They walked in and pressed the button for the Belmonts' floor. O'Riordan tapped his foot all the way up, much to the irritation of the other two men. Then the doors opened and they stepped out of the elevator. They strode purposefully towards the door of the apartment.

Which is when they heard the gunshot.

36

Bobbie and Nolan's first reaction upon seeing the lawyer pull a gun from his pocket was "you're kidding". This was as much a comment on the, rather ridiculous, figure the lawyer had cut since Bobbie had landed her bombshell accusation. After the first few moments of shock, the next thought occurred to both. This man, with the help of his wife, had already dispatched two people to that great lawyer's office in the sky and there was nothing in the eyes of Belmont that suggested they were beyond ensuring a few more people entered that waiting room.

Under any normal circumstances, Nolan would have considered trying to persuade someone holding a gun on him to consider the penal downsides involved with murder. The Belmonts were well beyond the pale on that score, so deaf ears awaited any plea.

'Take out your guns and put them on the table,' said Belmont to the two policemen. 'Any funny business and that broad you're so sweet on gets it.' The gun was now pointed, rather menacingly, as if it could be anything else, at Bobbie.

Oddly, and rather frustratingly for Bobbie, she was both petrified and elated by what the lawyer had both said and implied. She scolded herself for being delighted by the thought that Nolan might be attracted to her. It would all be rather for naught if Belmont pulled the trigger.

'Any bright ideas, guys?' asked Bobbie, hoping she sounded calmer than she felt. She saw Nolan reach into his pocket and take out a gun with his index finger and thumb and lay it on the table.

'That would be "no", then,' added Bobbie dryly.

'What can you possibly hope to gain?' asked Nolan. Behind him, Yeats had also put his gun on the floor. The two men put their hands up.

'I don't fancy the chair, nor does Olivia,' pointed out Belmont, which was a reasonable enough point supposed Nolan, but it did have one, rather glaring, flaw.

'Where will you go?' asked Bobbie, ever the journalist. As a human-interest angle she was intensely curious. She saw Nolan glance at her wryly.

'Telling you that would rather defeat the object of our escape, wouldn't you say, Miss Flynn?' replied Belmont.

'I daresay it would,' admitted Bobbie, a little defeated.

While all this was going on, Renat was standing immobile and impassive, unsure if he should raise his hands or try and do something about the situation. In truth, there was no side that was preferable to the other. He doubted Belmont would want to help him. In fact, the more he thought about it, the more he realised that he might want to put an end to their business association, permanently.

'What are you going to do?' asked Nolan. 'What can you do?'

'We could do away with you all and say that it was Renat who did this,' said Belmont.

The looks on the faces of Bobbie, Nolan and Yeats suggested that this would be stretching credibility beyond its natural tolerance limits.

'So you'll say you overpowered Renat, here?' suggested Nolan, contempt dripping from every syllable.

Belmont had the good grace to smile at this, but, then again, he was a gun to the good in this particular confrontation.

'Never bring sarcasm to a gunfight,' replied Belmont before chuckling at his own joke.

Bobbie's attention was distracted now, by something else. It was a consideration that had not yet been raised. Now was the time to do it.

'And what about Violet?' asked Bobbie.

'What about her?' said Belmont flippantly. This caused Olivia Belmont to frown a little.

'You're just going to leave her like that?' pressed Bobbie.

The sneer on Belmont's face was as cruel as anything Bobbie had ever seen. He said, 'Why not? It's not like she's our daughter.'

The timing of this statement could not have been more exquisitely awful for Belmont and Bobbie later felt a degree of guilt at having engineered it so.

'Papa?' said a voice from behind Belmont, coming from the corridor. Violet was standing in the doorway, open mouthed at the scene before her. Then she caught sight of Renat, to be fair, a six-foot six Russian man-mountain is rather difficult to miss and he was moving at great speed in the direction of the man holding a gun, whose attention had been momentarily taken up by the sound of the child's voice.

Renat smacked into Belmont just as the gun went off.

'Renat,' screamed Violet.

The Russian was now lying on top of, a well and truly flattened, Belmont. Nolan and Yeats were on Belmont in a moment lest he loose off another shot. This was unlikely, as the only thing the lawyer was going to discharge were the groans of man with several cracked ribs. Yeats grabbed the gun from Belmont's limp hand while Nolan gently rolled Renat off the lawyer's crushed body.

It was just at this point when the door crashed open causing Olivia Belmont to wake up from her shock and begin screaming.

Harrigan burst into the room followed by Fleischer. O'Riordan leapt in moments later, having ensured that his two men would be the first to get shot if a firefight erupted. The sight that greeted the new arrivals was uncommon, to say the least.

Two of his men appeared to be tending to a wounded kidnapper, the foster mother of the kidnap victim was screaming, the kidnap victim herself was crying, on behalf of the man who had kidnapped her and what on earth was that busybody daughter of Inspector Flynn doing in the room?

'What the hell is going on?' demanded O'Riordan. This, at least, had the virtue of halting Olivia Belmont's tears, if only because it sounded, for a moment, like her own husband had woken up from his state of unconsciousness.

The captain glared at Bobbie first and then turned his attention to the Russian, who had a patch of red evident even on his overcoat.

Instinctively O'Riordan pointed his gun at Renat. Nolan stared in disbelief at his captain. He said, 'This man needs a hospital.'

Bobbie was already over by the phone and calling for an ambulance. O'Riordan frowned and lowered his gun, disconsolately. There was nothing in the scene before him that suggested he was going to build his next promotion on this. It was a mess. Still, they had the child. Better still they had the kidnapper and best of all they had the mastermind of the crime. Perhaps it wouldn't be something that he could use personally for his career progression but, over time, the details of these cases became blurred. What remained was a track record of achievement and this was, after a fashion, a successful outcome for the captain.

An hour later, Renat the Russian was in hospital, being patched up. The bullet had been fired at such close range that it had passed through him.

Bobbie, at Nolan's request, was to stay with Violet until she was picked up and taken to the Roman Catholic Orphan Asylum. Violet had been away just over fourteen months. She was clearly distraught, at seeing her foster parents arrested. What made it worse for Bobbie was the stoic acceptance that her dream was over.

She no longer had a family.

'I'll go with her to the home,' offered Bobbie. O'Riordan grunted a form of acceptance to this, while Nolan nodded and gave a half-smile of gratitude. She went with Mrs Burley, to help Violet dress and pack. As they were doing this, the Belmonts were taken away to be charged with two murders and conspiracy to kidnap a minor. As they led the couple away, Inspector Flynn arrived at the apartment.

He took Nolan by the arm and led him to one side.

'Is my daughter here?' he asked the young detective. There was just a hint of anger on his face. Nolan nodded in the direction of the corridor leading to the bedrooms. The old detective's eyes hardened and he said in a snarled whisper, 'When this is over young man, you and I are going to have a short talk, about how she ended up here and how you like being in police uniform.'

There was nothing in there for Nolan, so he nodded and hurried to join the others in the hallway outside the apartment. He heard the sound of a bell and the elevator doors opening and closing.

It seemed symbolic. The end of a case and a day, as strange as any he had ever encountered. He was now alone in the living room. From another room he heard the sound of two women talking. There was also a child, he could tell from the occasional silences and the sound of crying.

There was a knock on the door which was still open. Flynn turned and saw there was a cab driver standing in the doorway. The man was about his age and smoking a cigar.

'You got another one of those? asked Flynn.

'Sorry bud, last one,' said the cabbie. 'I'm here to pick up a kid to bring her to the orphanage.'

Flynn heard the sound of sobs coming from one of the bedrooms. He had been a cop for four decades, but the sound of a child's heartbreak always got to him. He reached into his wallet and extracted a couple of dollars.

'Don't worry. Buy yourself a coffee.'

The cabbie departed, leaving Flynn to the silence of the empty room. A carriage clock ticked noisily over the mantelpiece. It echoed around the room which felt cavernous now that everyone had left. Outside, sirens began to wail, as the police took the Belmonts away. Flynn wandered over to the window to observe their departure.

Just then, Bobbie appeared in the living room with Violet. Flynn felt a flash of anger as he saw his daughter and the thought of what she had been through, the risks she had taken. Then he saw her red-rimmed eyes and those of the young girl beside her.

She fixed her eyes on her father, while fighting back tears and whispered, 'Don't say anything.'

So Flynn said nothing.

37

Midnight 3rd January 1922: Philadelphia

It was a cold and cramping Bugsy McDaid that alighted from his car, well, strictly speaking, someone else's car, at just after midnight, following the worst day of his life. Bugsy was not a man given to post-mortems on when things were wrong, especially when blame was easily apportioned. Elsewhere.

He was not to blame. That much was clear to him. It was the big Russian sap and, by extension, the woman who had hired him. Now he was the fall guy. To say he felt bitter about this is like saying General Custer was a little miffed at his scouts for not spotting a few thousand Sioux and Cherokee in their midst.

The journey from New York had been tortuous on so many levels, that even thinking about it provoked an attack of the heebie-jeebies. How he had made it in one piece without an accident, on the treacherous roads, never mind the constant presence of his old friend, anxiety, was anyone's guess.

However, he had made it. He was in Philly and he was outside his brother's apartment block. While they had never been very close, Pete was made of the right stuff. He was ten years older than Bugsy and had graduated from a life on the wrong side of the law to becoming reasonably legit. He worked in insurance.

Bugsy groaned as he stretched his aching limbs that had been frozen to the seat and working the pedals of the car. His hands had frostbite, of that he was certain and he couldn't feel the end of his nose. He was aching all over. He was starving and he would need a week to defrost.

The police intercepted him as he negotiated the icy steps, leading to the doors of his brother's apartment block.

'Bugsy McDaid,' said a big detective, flashing a gun at him to dissuade him from any funny business. 'You are under arrest for the kidnapping of a child...'

Bugsy looked at the detective and the three uniformed men who had appeared out of nowhere, and realised the game was up. He would return for another spell in Sing Sing. He put his hands up in response to the gun pointed at him.

'Put that away, I'll come quietly.'

'Good idea, Bugsy,' said the policeman.

'I don't suppose you got a sandwich or something?'

Bugsy climbed into the police car, that was parked around the corner and within moments he was whisked away to the sound of a siren.

At an upstairs window of the apartment block, a man wearing a rumpled blue shirt, open to the navel, went to the window of his apartment and looked out the window.

'What's going on Pete?' asked his wife, in a voice that could not have been less interested.

Pete McDaid turned to his wife Beverley and said, 'No idea. Probably the cops caught some kids messing around.'

The next morning, Renat the Russian found himself waking up in agony. His side hurt like hell. He moaned and then realised he was not alone in the hospital room. It smelled of antiseptic, had white walls and could not have been less conducive to recovery than if he had slept on a bed of nails and had witches screaming abuse at the patients.

Renat turned and saw a patrolman sitting by his bedside. The look on the cop's face was less than sympathetic. A nurse appeared in the room. She was pretty but, if anything, even less sympathetic looking than the cop.

'The patient is awake,' said the cop.

'So I see. When are you taking him away? We need the bed for someone who needs it,' said the nurse.

'We'll have him off your hands as soon as I get the word. Mid-morning at the latest.'

'What'll happen to him?' asked the nurse, in a voice that suggested a firing squad would be a sensible approach.

The policeman decided against going through the process that Renat would face and chose instead to cut to the chase.

'Lover-boy here will go to jail for a long time with any luck.'

A few hours later, Inspector Flynn faced a similar question from his daughter, as they sat in the car driving towards Hell's Kitchen. He sighed and considered how best to answer. Bobbie was in a strange mood. In some respects, she should have been feeling triumphant. She had helped crack the kidnapping case, a fact that did not bear thinking about for Flynn. She had filed a story that, for the third day running, had made the front page of the *New York American*.

Her star was rising yet she was in a moment of undisguised despondency. There were a number of reasons for this and Flynn was not going to help matters very much when he answered her.

'As the kidnapping victim is a child under 18 years of age and the alleged perpetrator is a stranger, rather than a family member, then the minimum sentence of incarceration in federal prison is around 20 years, honey.'

Bobbie was silent as she listened to this. Her attention was fixed on the world outside the window.

'If she hears that it will break her heart,' said Bobbie after a while.

'I know,' said Flynn, and once more considered the, rather odd, relationship that had been forged in the fire of the kidnapping hell between Violet and the Russian.

'Will the court take into account the fact that he was trying to return her?'

This prompted another sigh and Flynn answered carefully, 'They may not accept her testimony, or even call her in the first place.'

'Even a statement read out in court?'

'That's what I mean, they may not accept that,' replied Flynn. He paused for a moment and then added, 'Look Bobbie, you can't ignore the fact that he kidnapped the girl in the first place.'

'What will you ask the prosecutor to do?'

'His job, Bobbie,' said Flynn gently. 'Look, our system of justice isn't perfect. If Renat were some rich guy, I'm sure all sorts of mitigations would come into play. Your story might help influence things and I will add my bit, but Renat has to face justice. He has to, otherwise where are we?'

Where are we indeed, thought Bobbie? She was staring out the window at kids playing in the street in rags and in shoes that were falling apart. Some stared back at her as they passed her.

'Nearly there,' said Flynn, turning down into a street that was, if anything even more desolate than the one they had driven on. Despite the cold, the street was mobbed with people. And these people, in Flynn's eyes, were composed of vagrants, petty thieves and prostitutes. He hated to be here and he hated even more that he was with his daughter.

They drew up outside a tenement building, that looked as if its collapse was imminent. The police car attracted a number of people over and Flynn felt an overwhelming urge to call the whole thing off and drive away.

Bobbie was shocked by the dirty faces of the children, pushed against the window of the car. The grime seemed to be like a tattoo, rather than something that could be washed away by soap and water.

'You sure about this?' asked Flynn gently.

Bobbie steeled herself and looked at her father in the eye, 'I'm sure. We have to try.'

They alighted from the car and Flynn addressed the crowd of boys.

'Okay boys, this is how it's going to be. Who is the leader here?'

A boy stepped forward without much prompting from the others, He was probably no more than twelve, but the hard face and eyes that met Flynn's, were much older. He was taller than the others, but just as skinny. His clothes were too small for him and had been so a year ago.

'Name, son,' asked Flynn, addressing him as if he was an adult.

'Billy,' replied the boy.

Flynn pointed to the tenement building. And then fixed a penetrating don't-mess-with-me stare on the boy.

'You seem like a public-spirited boy, son. Now, my daughter and I are going into that building over there. When we come back out, I want this car in the same condition in which I left it. Understand?'

The boy nodded but said nothing.

'Give me your hand on that,' said Flynn. He held out his hand.

The boy shook it and then found that he had a quarter in his hand. The boy looked at it and then back at Flynn. He did not seem so impressed.

'There'll be three more of those if you keep your end of the deal.'

The boy nodded once. The contract had been struck. Flynn turned and motioned to Bobbie to follow behind him. Bobbie ignored this, of course, and walked alongside him into the dingy redbrick building.

They walked up two flights of stairs, until they came to the third-floor corridor. Flynn sighed at the sight and smell that greeted them. It was night dark because the window had so much dust and grime. The smell that assaulted them was the very worst that humanity could offer. It was the kind of place that rats might refuse to live in, due to the unhealthy conditions.

Flynn went to the first door and gave it a rap.

'Who is it?' shouted a woman. 'I ain't finished yet.'

'I'm looking for Eddie Scott,' shouted Flynn.

'Who's looking?' asked the woman, her voice full of suspicion.

'NYPD. Open up, we want to talk to Eddie Scott, said Flynn before adding what he hoped would be a mollifying clarification, 'Eddie's done nothin' wrong.' Flynn suspected this was stretching credulity a little far and would be seen this way by those inside.

Much to his surprise, a minute later, the door opened a few inches. A woman peaked out. She was wearing a dressing gown and Flynn doubted not much else. Her eyes flicked from Flynn to Bobbie.

'Why are you here?' asked the woman though the crack in the doorway. She folded her arms across her chest like a doorman refusing entry at a speakeasy.

'May we come in?' asked Bobbie. 'It's about Violet.'

'Eddie,' screeched the woman, in a voice that was a likely explanation for the wallpaper peeling off the walls. 'They want to talk to you about Violet.'

A noise from a door behind the woman provided a none too positive feeling about how welcome Bobbie and Flynn would be. Sure enough, a man appeared who would not be described by any parent of a daughter as a "keeper". He was tall, thin and gave every impression of having done time. He walked with a certain bravado, but his eyes were furtive, perpetually shifting, as if searching for an opportunity that would always elude him.

'What's she done now?' asked the father of Violet, searching for something in his trousers.

Moments later, the door behind Eddie opened and a man appeared, half-dressed, who was twenty pounds past the point that demarcated obesity from merely "big boned". He yelled angrily down the corridor, 'Hey what's the big idea? I didn't pay good money for this.'

Bobbie turned to her father and shook her head.

Just over a minute later they were back on the street in front of the tenement. The kids were still surrounding the car, but it looked to be in one piece. Flynn glanced towards his daughter. She had been silent all the way down the stairs. This was ominous.

Reaching the boys, Flynn took some quarters out of his pocket and handed them to the boy who he knew as Billy. Nothing was said. The deal was completed on a nod. Flynn climbed back into the car. He looked at the grim set of his daughter's face and knew what was on her mind.

'No,' he said. Then, realising this was too brutal he added, 'Honey, we can't. It's madness.'

Bobbie turned to him with a look that he'd seen long before she was born, a look that belonged to another woman he'd loved and lost far too soon. The look told him he was in the wrong fight, with the wrong person and on the wrong side.

Epilogue

Roman Catholic Orphan Asylum, New York: 7th January 1922

The Roman Catholic Orphan Asylum was an imposing redbrick set of buildings that overlooked the Harlem River from a ridge nearly two hundred feet above tidewater. There were two buildings—one for boys, the other for girls.

The dining room for the girls, was a cavernous affair, high ceiling and enormous windows through which a celestial light streamed onto the tables.

Violet sat on her own away from the other girls in the dining room. She was one of the oldest children and, while she did not always prefer her own company, today was one of those days when the others knew to leave her alone. Many had known her from before she had left, while for others, she was just a new kid. There was a turnover in the home as many kids found new places to live. For an unfortunate few, this would never happen.

Some kids were just too difficult. The staff had worried that Violet would fall into just such a category. Her circumstances had been among the most squalid when she arrived three years previously. She had taken to life in the home much more quickly than anyone could have predicted. Yet, while far from being an easy child, she was not unpopular, but there was a distance between her and the other children and even with the teachers.

Once she had been equipped with the basics of literacy, she took it upon herself to learn, spending hours in the library, on her own. The Asylum had become her home and she much preferred it to what she had come from or, indeed, where she might end up.

Her unwillingness to engage with potential foster parents or seeming desire not to leave the safety of the home, made the decision of the Belmonts to foster her something of a surprise. This was as nothing to the shock they felt when they heard about their arrest a few days earlier and Violet's return.

Unlike the other children, she was a voracious reader. It had always been so. Denied the chance to read, while she was the daughter of Eddie and Sadie Scott, it was as if a bottle of champagne had been uncorked. Her reading and writing had improved at a spectacular rate while she attended the school run by the nuns.

Following her departure from the home, to live with the Belmonts, she had attended a private school where her natural intelligence, allied to a desire to please her foster parents, had driven her to even greater efforts to learn.

Violet sat alone at the dining table, reading a newspaper, while eating. Fitzroy Belmont had often done this at breakfast, commenting on the latest things happening on Wall Street. Even then, Violet could see that Olivia Belmont wasn't the least bit interested in what he was saying. Yet, her heart ached for those mornings.

Her initial suspicions, about leaving the home, had been wiped away when she saw the apartment that she would live in.

The sight of her bedroom with its beautiful bed, the soft pillows, and the dolls had convinced her she had found her dream home. It was a world away from Hell's Kitchen.

Yet that was all it was. A dream.

What she would have given to be back in that apartment listening to a monologue on the subject of stocks and shares, from her foster father. What she would have given to see her foster mother's bored expression. Her chest tightened as she read about the story. Her story, in the newspapers.

She read about their story, too.

Thankfully, there were no pictures of her in the papers as that would have been the final humiliation. She was relieved also that they had refrained from saying into which home she had been placed. Yet, her degradation and desolation was being laid bare, every day, in the newspapers. How her caring foster parents had been transformed, almost overnight, into a grasping, murderous couple who had used her to become closer to the Monk family.

Her life in Hell's Kitchen had instilled in her a hardness, that manifested itself in a refusal to show emotion, or even to cry. The year with the Belmonts had softened her, because now she cried every night, when the lights went out. Mute tears, the sound of her sobbing muffled by the pillow that fooled no one in her dormitory. They all knew she was suffering, but they knew also that nothing could be done.

She stayed at the table long after the other children had gone out to play. The sounds of their laughter filtered through to her from the playground outside. Violet, however, was lost in the newsprint, pouring over her story and then, for old times' sake, glancing at the pages her foster father had read about the markets.

So lost was she in reading that she did not hear the sound of Sister Assumpta Coughlan, arrive at her table. Sister Assumpta was in her fifties. She had joined the Sisters of Mercy at the age of eighteen. From Violet's first days in the institution, Sister Assumpta had taken an interest in the young girl. She had felt the joy in seeing her young charge develop an interest in reading; she'd experienced a strange mixture of sorrow and gladness when Violet had found a home. Her return and the palpable sense of loss the young girl bore, was heart-breaking to Sister Assumpta.

'Violet,' said Sister Assumpta, gently. 'May I speak to you for a moment?'

Violet looked up and sketched a smile for the nun. Sister Assumpta took Violet's hand. She glanced down at the paper and smiled, 'How are your shares performing?'

Violet grinned and replied, 'I'll soon be able to buy this place.' Then Violet frowned for a moment. She could see that the nun was struggling with her emotions. It was bad enough that she felt desolate, she didn't want this dear woman to feel as she did. Sister Assumpta had been the one reason that had made Violet want to stay at the home, when the Belmonts had first expressed an interest in fostering her.

'What's wrong?' asked Violet putting her other hand on Sister Assumpta's.

Sister Assumpta's eyes welled up with tears. She smiled gamely and said, 'Violet, there's someone here to see you. I think, well, I think that you should speak with them.'

She saw something in the nun's eyes, but it only made her shake her head. She could not speak. Violet's eyes glistened with tears. She looked away. She could not bear to reveal weakness.

'Violet, I think you should speak to them.'

Violet turned to Sister Assumpta. While there were tears in her eyes, there was something else too and Violet, who could read people like she read the newspaper, recognised what she was seeing.

It was hope.

Sister Assumpta stood to one side, allowing Violet to look across the dining room to the doorway. There were two people standing there. She recognised the young woman with the auburn hair. Beside her was a man, the young woman's father, she remembered. They'd taken her back to the girls' home that awful night.

Violet's eyes flicked back to the nun. She didn't know what to say. How to frame the question that was on her mind. Yet, the question contained only one word.

Why?

'I think you should speak to them Violet. They seem nice,' prompted Sister Assumpta.

Violet was fighting a losing battle with her emotions but fight she did. Traitorous tears tricked down her cheeks. Her body heaved with the sobs that she was struggling to suppress. Violet felt Sister Assumpta grip her hand tightly. She was nodding to her.

'Are you sure about this?' asked Flynn, for what might have been the tenth time. His daughter turned to him and he immediately felt remorse. This was a man's fate, however. To question, to challenge and then to accept before the guilt set in.

Yet, it was madness what Bobbie was contemplating. He wasn't wrong to think this or even say so. But then wasn't life full of such folly? Nancy had been the love of his life, a wealthy socialite who had gone against her family's wishes and married a young cop who had saved her life. What would his life had been had he not known someone prepared to do the unthinkable?

Bobbie's eyes were unwavering and he nodded to her and even managed a smile.

'You're so like your mother,' said Flynn and, as ever with men, he made it sound like both an insult as well as the greatest compliment he could pay anyone.

It made Bobbie smile though and, oddly, gave her courage because at that moment it was failing her. What was she doing? How could she even contemplate upending this young girl's life that had careered from one nightmare to another without pause to wake up and breathe in the morning air?

Even from across the room, Bobbie could see the torment on the young girl's face. She knew the home was a refuge, of sorts, for Violet. It even occurred to Bobbie that the young girl might simply say, 'no.' She could hardly be blamed for having lost trust with the world outside the walls of this girls' home. Here she was safe, while the world outside had shown her nothing but depravity and violence.

Bobbie saw the young girl rise up from her seat slowly. Uncertainty was written across her face. Perhaps fear also. She was still gripping the hand of the nun. Violet looked up at the nun who nodded to her.

Bobbie turned to her father. He managed to make a frown look like a smile.

'Well, go on. Talk to her,' he said, gruffly. 'What are you waiting for?'

The End

Research Notes

This is a work of fiction. However, it references real-life individuals. Gore Vidal, in his introduction to Lincoln, writes that placing history in fiction or fiction in history has been unfashionable since Tolstoy and that the result can be accused of being neither. He defends the practice, pointing out that writers from Aeschylus to Shakespeare to Tolstoy have done so with, not inconsiderable, success and merit.

I have mentioned a number of key real-life individuals and events in this novel. My intention, in the following section, is to explain a little more about their connection to this period and this story.

New York American
The New York American Journal, a morning newspaper, was founded by the brother of Joseph Pulitzer, Albert, in 1882. The newspaper was acquired by William Randolph Hearst in 1896. He renamed the paper, *The New York American* in 1901. It eventually merged with its sister evening paper, The New York Evening Journal in 1937. It was based in the New York Tribune building in Park Street. For a long time its star reporter was Damon Runyon.

Damon Runyon (1880 – 1946)

Damon Runyon is one of the greatest American writers of the early 20th century and certainly its most famous newspaper journalist. Although famous now for being the author of short stories 'On Broadway' which later became the basis for the Frank Sinatra / Marlon Brando musical *"Guys and Dolls"*, Runyon had already become firmly established as a newspaperman on the New York American and was its best paid writer. His articles, on baseball and boxing, made him a must read for a paper that had a circulation of millions. He started with the Hearst newspapers in 1911.

However, it is for his stories of Broadway that he is best remembered. He began to publish them in the thirties. They feature many thinly disguised portraits of the hustlers, gangsters, actors and gamblers that he associated with. His ear for the Broadway vernacular became known as "Runyonese": a mixture of formal speech and colourful slang, which was usually in the present tense, without any contractions.

Arthur Rothstein (1882 – 1928)

Arnold Rothstein was nicknamed "The Brain" and was one of the first American racketeers to take advantage of the business opportunity represented by Prohibition. He became leader of the Jewish mob in New York City and was widely reputed to have organised corruption in professional athletics, including fixing the 1919 World Series. He was reputed to have been a mentor of future crime bosses Lucky Luciano,

Meyer Lansky, Frank Costello, Bugsy Siegel and numerous others.

Roman Catholic Orphan Asylum

The Roman Catholic Benevolent Society, established in 1817, was the oldest charitable institution in the Archdiocese of New York. At that time, parent-less Catholic children were lost to the faith if they were taken in by Protestant orphan societies. They established an orphanage for Catholic children. Over the century it moved to several locations as the numbers grew, before moving from mid-town Manhattan to the Bronx.

Prohibition (1920 – 1933)

The basic facts of prohibition barely tell the extraordinary impact on American society. The 18th Amendment ended the production, sale, import and transportation of alcohol, nationwide. The law drove many Americans to hoard alcohol or become de facto criminals by consuming illicit booze created by criminal gangs and often sold through illegal bars called speakeasies.

The law ended with the ratification of the 21st Amendment, in 1933. This ended one of the more extraordinary and, arguably, self-defeating initiatives in American history as it gave rise and strength to various criminal gangs, particularly the Italian American Mafia, led by men such as Al Capone.

About the Author

Jack Murray was born in Northern Ireland but has spent over half his life living just outside London, except for some periods spent in Australia, Monte Carlo, and the US.

An artist, as well as a writer, Jack's work features in collections around the world and he has exhibited in Britain, Ireland, and Monte Carlo.

A spin off series from the Kit Aston novels was published in 2020 featuring Aunt Agatha as a young woman solving mysterious murders.

Another spin off series is features Inspector Jellicoe. It is set in the late 1950's/early 1960's.

Jack finished work on a World War II trilogy in 2022. The three books look at the war from both the British and the German side. They have been published through Lume Books and are available on Amazon.

If you enjoyed meeting the character Bobbie Flynn, then you may be interested to learn that a new spin off series featuring this character and her father will be out in 2024.

Acknowledgements

It is not possible to write a book on your own. There are contributions from so many people either directly or indirectly over many years. Listing them all would be an impossible task.

Special mention therefore should be made to my wife and family who have been patient and put up with my occasional grumpiness when working on this project.

My brother, Edward, has helped in proofing and made supportive comments that helped me tremendously. Thank you, too, Debra Cox, David Sinclair, Nathalie Pettus and Anna Wietrzychowska who have been a wonderful help in reducing the number of irritating errors that have affected my earlier novels. A word of thanks to Charles Gray and Brian Rice who have provided legal and accounting support.

My late father and mother both loved books. They encouraged a love of reading in me. In particular, they liked detective books, so I must tip my hat to the two greatest writers of this genre, Sir Arthur and Dame Agatha.

Following writing, comes the business of marketing. My thanks to Mark Hodgson and Sophia Kyriacou for their advice on this important area. Additionally, a shout out to the wonderful folk on 20Booksto50k.

Finally, my thanks to the teachers who taught and nurtured a love of writing.

Printed in Great Britain
by Amazon